THE
HAIR
WREATH

AND OTHER STORIES

HALLI VILLEGAS

ChiZine Publications

FIRST EDITION

The Hair Wreath and Other Stories © 2010 by Halli Villegas
Jacket artwork © 2010 by Erik Mohr
All Rights Reserved.

LIBRARY AND ARCHIVES CANADA CATALOGUING IN PUBLICATION

Villegas, Halli
  The hair wreath : and other stories / Halli Villegas.

ISBN 978-1-926851-02-0

  I. Title.

PS8593.I3894H35 2010   C813'.6   C2010-903131-8

CHIZINE PUBLICATIONS
Toronto, Canada
www.chizinepub.com
info@chizinepub.com

Edited by Sandra Kasturi
Copyedited by Gemma Files
Proofread by Shirarose Wilensky

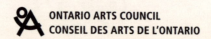

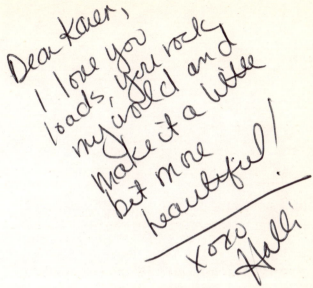

Dear Karen,
I love you
loads, you rock
my world and
make it a little
bit more
beautiful!
xoxo Halli

For David and Misha

THE
HAIR
WREATH

AND OTHER STORIES

Table of Contents

The Hair Wreath

They had to get out of the city. Their loft, which they had finally bought after many deprivations in the form of forgoing dinner out and Starbucks lattés for two years, was stifling. Despite exposed brick walls, floor-to-ceiling windows and proximity to all the city's amenities, it had no outside access. No balconies marred the front of this genuine industrial building. The floor-to-ceiling windows that had been such a selling point in January let in relentless light in July.

Standing only in her bikini underwear in the middle of the loft, she said, "We should have taken the place with central air."

A sheen of sweat brought out the blonde down along her arms.

"We wanted the exposed brick," he said from the depths of a leather recliner where he sat naked. "Remember, we talked about it?" There was a sucking sound of flesh unsticking from leather as he shifted in his chair.

"Yes, yes, we talked, but who knew the goddamn windows would be so hard to cover?"

They had only managed to rig curtains about halfway up; neither was very handy and they couldn't afford to have it done professionally. She crossed over to him and sat in his lap.

"I'm not mad at you." She nestled her head into his shoulder. Her short blonde hair rubbed against his neck.

"Too hot." He pushed her off. "Let's go for a drive. Out of this city."

She tossed her head to settle her cap of hair back in place. "Alright." She was already walking toward the bathroom. "But I get the shower first."

The acrid scent of her blonde sweat lingered in the air as he listened to her turn on the water. He lay back in the leather chair, enjoying the easily remedied discomfort of his damp body against the slick surface.

For fun, they took a back road off of the main highway. The city was twenty minutes behind. They turned the radio on loudly and sang along. All the car's windows were open and the wind whipped their voices away, but every once in a while she reached over and squeezed his hand. He turned and smiled at her, his palm briefly cupping her thigh. Lifted by the breeze, her hair made a glinting halo. His hair had dried quickly, the heat making it curl up at the ends. She wrapped a curl around her finger and smoothed it down flat on his neck as he drove.

Just after an old stone bridge that crossed a creek, they came to a small town. The houses were Victorian for the most part, set back from the road by wide lawns. Occasionally a wartime bungalow appeared; then the Victorian next to it would have a truncated lot, the larger house brooding over the smaller.

They joked about how they would buy one of these houses when they made their first million. Their country place. They looked at each other, still laughing, and felt it was entirely possible.

The little main street of the town had a white clapboard café with ruffled curtains where they stopped for lunch.

"This is the perfect day in the country," she said over a glass of homemade iced tea. Her face glowed. He reached across the table and touched her hand. Her hair fell across her flushed cheeks as she bent over his hand and kissed it.

After lunch, they wandered up the few blocks of the main street. They looked in the window of the dusty hardware store, and the clothing store with the headless mannequins wearing sweatshirts that featured baskets of kittens or flowers.

"Ready to go back to the car?"

"Alright," she said, taking his hand, but something across the street caught her eye.

"An antique store." Her voice was excited. "Let's go see if they have anything for the loft."

She crossed and he followed, though he was tired, and the thought of the drive back was beginning to weigh on him.

A bell on the store's door jangled into the moted air. It was several degrees cooler in the shop. His nostrils flared, recognizing the papery, dry smell of old things. A woman with a long grey braid and a pilled lavender t-shirt watched them from behind a glass counter.

"Howdy," he said, raising a hand to her. She nodded, then looked back down at the paper she had spread out on the counter top.

His wife had already begun to dig through the shop like a little terrier, her white tennis shoes shining among the heaps of old furniture and listing piles of junk. He picked up a few pieces of glass with knobs on them like glass boils.

He fingered through a tin box of old photos. Dumpy looking women in voluminous dark dresses, heavy hair wound in braids or swathed around their unsmiling faces. To him, the eyes in these old photos always looked blank, empty, as if the unchecked disease or early capricious death of the era had made them into unfeeling automatons. He imagined them pushing out one child after another to replace those that died young, burying their feelings deeper with each successive death. He dropped the photos back into the box and tried to wipe the black dirt from his fingers on the hem of his shorts.

He was about to wait outside in the sun when his wife called to him. She was holding a yellowed cardboard box. Inside, on a pile of tissue, was a shallow shadow box with a faded velvet background. On the velvet was a wreath. It had fibrous-looking flowers with centres of glass beads. Fragile circlets sprouted at various intervals. The whole thing had a dull sheen to it, the colours ranging from dark brown to ashy yellow. He put one finger out and touched it. The texture was unmistakable.

"It's hair." He rubbed his hand violently on his shirt. The skin crept up the back of his knees.

"Isn't it fantastic? It's a hair wreath. I've *always* wanted one." She brushed her bangs off her forehead with one hand. There was a black streak along one of her cheeks.

"They were in remembrance, of friends, lovers, family. The dead and the living." She looked down into the box smiling. "I've always wanted one."

"No."

She looked up, surprised.

"It's awful, dead people's hair. God, it makes me shudder just to think of it."

She narrowed her eyes. "You're being silly. It's artwork. It's an antique. It will look wonderful on the brick wall in the loft."

He shook his head. "Not in my house."

"Your house?"

The proprietress came over. He could see now that her silver plait reached to her waist.

"Find something?"

She took the box. He watched his wife's face go still. He knew she was wondering if the woman would set the price too high if she saw excitement on her face.

"Oh, the hair wreath. Bought that at an estate sale over to Kirkfield. Used to be you couldn't give them away, now they're hard to find. Seems they've become collectible." She chuckled and handed the box back to his wife.

"How much do you want for it?" his wife asked, fitting the lid back on the box.

The shop owner hesitated. A ray of light filtered through the filthy windows and lit his wife's hair into gold. She held the box close to her chest, her arms crossed over it.

The proprietress shrugged. "Let's say a hundred, no tax."

"I'll take it." His wife didn't look at him as she followed the shopkeeper to the front to pay.

That night she had him sink an anchor into the brick wall to hang the wreath from. He didn't argue, knowing that he couldn't win, but he refused to touch the thing. She could hang it herself. He went to take another shower, wanting to get the day's dirt off his skin.

After his shower he bent to clean the hair catch in the drain. Twined in it were her bright hairs and his dark ones, curled together wet and slick from the water and soap. He left it there, and closed the shower curtain.

The loft's windows were not totally dark as the city lights filtered in, but deep grey, with nothing behind them. The heat of the day still filled the open space and he felt the relief of the shower evaporating in the muggy air. Naked, he got into bed. In the half-light he could still see the hair wreath's intricate spirals and trembling flowers.

She was asleep next to him, breathing steadily, her hair fanned out on the pillow like a silk tassel. He closed his eyes to block out the wreath, the dusty shop, the day, and slipped into sleep.

When he woke later into the half-dark of the loft, a woman in a black silk dress bent over him. Her full skirts swayed as she hovered in the close air. Around her head were wound thick dark braids. Her eyes were empty, pale grey. He lay still, hoping she would believe he was asleep. She reached up and unpinned her braids. They uncoiled with the dry sound of snakes gliding through the burnt stubble of summer grass. She began to comb them out with her fingers until they became a fall of dark water. She leaned closer and he was covered in her hair's smothering weight. The musty odour of long-dead forgotten people rose from the rippling strands. He cried out.

"Shh, shh—" His wife was beside him stroking his hair. She began to kiss him and then stretched her body over his. Her short hair brushed his cheek as she bent her mouth to his again. They moved together silently in the heat. Her scent, blonde and grassy, mingled with the musk of their lovemaking, but underneath he could detect the smell of things that hadn't seen the sun in a long time. When they finished, she collapsed on his chest, taking his breath away, her hair stinging where it touched his skin.

Over the shuddering crescent of her shoulder, he could see the hair wreath hanging on the loft's wall—half shadowed, half illuminated in the diluted city light.

D in the Underworld

They stare at her the minute she gets on the bus. D, refusing to be taken in by their challenge, takes the seat directly across from them, even though more than half the seats are empty. She is too old to be intimidated by teenagers. The girl has green hair. Spring green, the colour of new grass. Which means, D knows, that it was originally blonde. Dark hair bleached to take the colour would be spottier, less pure. The boy has straight blond hair that falls over one eye—a pretty face, but hard. For some reason D has always been suspicious of blond men. They strike her as sinister, concealing something behind smiles and light eyes. This is no man, though; he is a boy. Certainly, she has nothing to fear from a boy in a frayed oxford shirt, tie almost undone. He is also wearing grey flannel pants and Doc Martens. School uniform. D, who has only glanced at them when she first sat down, busies herself with her bag. Opens it to arrange crumpled Kleenex, ticket handy should a Toronto Transit operator board and ask to see it. Maybe they are brother and sister, with that blond hair; she glances again. The girl is looking at her. As if reading her thoughts, the girl leans over toward the boy and begins to kiss him, her hands running across his lap while he holds her thin shoulders.

Guess not. D looks at her bag again and snaps it shut. Outside the bus window the unlovely city flashes by. Out here, away from the city's core, there are strip malls, bungalows meant to look like trim cottages, but instead fronting on the busy street with litter on their lawns, and paint peeling from the quaint trim around their roof peaks. Towering above them, blank apartment buildings. D tries to imagine them new in 1960, 1970, when they weren't so soot-dimmed, their balconies rusted, hung with six-month-old Christmas lights, garbage banked along their steps among misshapen shrubs. She can't do it, not in this rain. Spring has been a long time coming this year, days of promise dissolving into this endless rain.

A group of schoolgirls runs for the bus stop, laughing, but they don't make it. This driver has no pity, and won't wait for the beauty of their long legs and flushed cheeks. Instead the doors close; the bus lurches forward, indifferent to their waving hands and calls. Despite herself, D cranes her neck around, looking for Stephanie, to see if she can spot her red coat in the midst of the girls. But their backs are to her now, and there is no red coat.

"Got a light?"

It's the boy across the aisle. He's holding a cigarette between two fingers, the girl curled around him; rather like a grass snake, D thinks, with that green hair.

"No. You're not allowed to smoke on the bus."

The boy looks at her. The mother in D rises.

"Besides, it's not good for you."

The boy flips his hair out of his eyes, but it falls right back with a fluid motion.

"The bus?" he asks, widening his eyes in mock innocence.

D gives the inevitable answer; it pulls from her tongue like taffy.

"No, smoking."

He laughs and so does D this time—letting herself not be offended, but easy as an adult might be with a cheeky teenager.

The girl seems to have fallen asleep, her mouth slightly open against the boy's arm.

"Coming from school?" D asks.

"Nope. Job interview," the boy says. He puts the cigarette behind his ear and shifts so his arm is around the girl.

D is surprised. A job interview—he doesn't look old enough to be out of school. One of the things with getting older is that the lower ages seem to blur together. Perhaps he is a dropout, not going to university—like D herself, though that is much more unusual here than in the States where she grew up. Then she had Stephanie, which made it impossible to go back, back especially to the mindset that seemed necessary for university—of being unencumbered, thinking of what you would like, only of yourself.

The boy is watching her, stroking the green hair of his girl absentmindedly.

"Did you get the job?"

"Not the Tim Horton's type. When they asked if I had ever tried their product and what I thought of it, I said you couldn't pay me to put that shit in my body." He smiles at D, expecting a rebuke, but she lets the automatic answer go.

"I suppose you had a cigarette right after?"

"Damn right."

They both laugh again, and the girl on his arm stirs.

"What's so funny?"

"Just talking about my job interview." He bends over her and kisses her forehead. She sits up and stretches.

"Oh God, that was a mistake. You at Tim Horton's, I can see it now. Hey, we're almost at our stop."

D looks out the window, only a few more stops until her own. Back here, downtown again, the streets are a bit more vibrant—boutiques, galleries, brownstones with brass numbers—but the rain is relentless. The bus shudders to a stop.

HALLI VILLEGAS

The boy snatches something out of his canvas satchel as he stands, drops it into her lap as he and the girl make their way to the doors, he guiding her with a hand at the small of her back. He turns, just as they are stepping off.

"Come if you can, it'll be fun."

D drops the paper into her bag and rides the last three stops to her house, watching out the window for Stephanie's red coat.

The apartment is empty. Ground floor of a three-storey row house; tiny hall, high ceiling, narrow rooms that lead one off the other. D drops her purse on the couch, blond wood and beige cushions, the cheapest IKEA had to offer. She bumps against the trash-picked coffee table, strewn with magazines and one burnt-down candle in a heavy silver holder. She goes into the kitchen to make tea. While the kettle boils, D closes herself in the tiny bathroom off the kitchen. She pees, and as she washes her hands in the sink afterwards, looks at herself in the mirror.

Why had that boy talked to her? Just fucking with her.

D sees her face as always. The slowly growing radius of fine lines around her eyes, the skin on her cheeks a little taut but rough with pores, hair—oh, that is the worst—brown, sere, carelessly pulled back. The brown turtleneck and pants, blunt nails, ugly shoes; no colour anywhere, drab as the day. She raises her hands to her cheeks and pulls them tight. Only thirty-three, but old, older than dirt. She lets her face go and goes back to the kitchen where her kettle is whistling, frantic at being forgotten.

D sits on the couch, mug balanced on a pile of old *Toronto Life* magazines stacked on the coffee table in front of her. She pulls her purse toward her and reaches in for the paper the boy dropped in her lap. It's an invitation, hand-lettered, printed on a copier.

Party tonight at the Underground. Doors open ten o'clock. Special appearance by Cerberus. Everyone will be there.

There is a crude drawing of some sort at the bottom. D can't make it out, a man poling a boat full of people on a river, or a crowd watching a band?

Great, now I need glasses too.

D drops it on the floor with a bunch of back issues of *Now* that she has to put out for recycling. She lays her head back against the couch and closes her eyes.

The front door bangs.

"Mom, I'm home."

D comes out of the kitchen as Stephanie walks into the living room, her dark hair flowing over the red coat they bought together that fall. D feels absolute joy, seeing her daughter's beauty and hearing her voice.

"Oh, Stephanie, you're home."

Stephanie tosses her knapsack on the couch. "I'm going to change." She heads for her room.

Unthinking, D slips into the familiar cadences. "Steph, take your bag with you."

Her daughter grabs the bag with a theatrical sigh and goes into her room, shutting the door. The radio comes on, something incoherent and loud. D stands listening for a moment. *Why am I standing here grinning like an idiot? I better start dinner.*

During dinner, Stephanie tells a school story whose only interest for D lies in the verve and intensity with which Stephanie lays out the intricate plot, describes her friends' characters, the importance she gives to something outside of her home, somewhere her mother can't go.

I love you, I love you, I love you, D thinks, watching her.

After dinner Stephanie says she is going to Alice's for the night. Alice around the block, Alice, who has a new CD she, Stephanie, covets and her own phone in her room. D is disappointed, had hoped they could watch a movie together or something, but Stephanie is growing up—can't be held to home any longer, is in high school this year which means at least boys, hopefully nothing else, nothing worse. D thinks of the boy on the bus, smoking, just rebellion, but still. D lets her go, sits on the couch while Stephanie packs. Turns on the TV, a little hurt despite her best intentions and the books she has carefully read, highlighting key points, describing the importance of the peer group in these years. Stephanie kisses her goodbye and shrugs into her red coat—and like a black wave D remembers, but Stephanie is at the door.

"Don't go, for Christ's sake, please Stephanie, don't go."

D can't seem to move off the couch, her limbs are leaden.

"See you tomorrow, Mom."

Please God, please God, let her not go. But the door closes and D is left crying on the couch—the ringing telephone pulling her out of the dream, tears still choking her voice as she answers.

It is the sergeant who has been working on Stephanie's case. They may have a lead. Someone may have seen her that night.

"Alone," D asks, wanting it so. "Was she alone?"

The sergeant clears his throat. "No, I'm sorry, with a man."

A few more words, he'll call with more later, they are following up immediately on the lead. D replaces the phone.

She stands in front of Stephanie's door. She has not been in this room since that night. The detectives have; they took Stephanie's journal with the white kitten on the front and a sheaf of other papers, letters passed in school about boys and sleepovers mostly. D opens the door, stands in the middle of the room, breath coming rapidly, breathing in the stale smell that only faintly still holds the scent of Stephanie.

Why did she ever let Stephanie have this front bedroom? It was bigger, yes, than the one in the back, but it faces the street. Did he watch her? Despite the heavy purple star-strewn curtains, did he see in? Why did she let Stephanie wear that pink lip gloss, the one that smells like candy? And why the hell had she let her walk the few blocks to Alice's alone.

"Come back," D calls into the empty room, pictures of puppies staring at her from the walls above the bed, watching her break down. "Come back, oh please God, I'll be so good, oh please make it go back."

She has to get out of the room. She'll tear her hair out if she doesn't. She is not the only one waiting— the room is waiting too, all things suspended without the person that chose them to reflect her personality, who gave them life.

D turns to the door, a poster for a band sloppily tacked there: a picture of a three-headed dog. Cerberus, the CD Alice had. A date, a time, a place. D tears it off the door and leaves Stephanie's waiting room.

D wears black. On the sidewalk in front of the club a few people stand or sit against walls. They too are dressed in black and their faces are pale under the streetlights. Talking low amongst themselves, they pass the small glow of a cigarette back and forth. D finds them peculiarly silent, no fresh bursts of laughter or the loud confident conversation that she associates with the young, particularly if they have been drinking.

D herself has had nothing to eat or drink. Since Stephanie disappeared, her appetite has been nothing. Most nights she dumps her plate of food untouched into the garbage under the sink, takes a sleeping pill and staggers to bed. Her work has given her leave. She is the administrative coordinator for a group of filmmakers. Being artists, they pride themselves on feeling another's pain, running a model workplace, unlike cold, corporate culture. But the last time one of them called to see how she was, D thought she detected impatience, or even boredom with the unchanging story, the misery that seems so overdramatic because it cannot be imagined by those outside. Most days D spends riding public transit all over the city, searching for Stephanie, letting everything else die.

The club has double doors of ragged wood with

heavy iron handles. It's guarded by a doorman—over six feet tall, black, and bald. He opens the door for D, but doesn't smile or meet her eyes. It's as if he sees right through her. Inside is almost impenetrable, the only light from dim yellow fixtures meant to look like torches bolted to the walls. There is a staircase down directly in front of her. The edges of the stairs have reflective tape on them, but still it is treacherous, the stairs hollowed in the centre from years of people descending. Everything is painted matte black, so there is no sense of the width of the staircase. D hugs the wall as she starts down. People pass her going both ways, brush against her—but again, as if she is invisible, no one says a word to her. She sees a brighter light inching up the bottom steps, like a fire casting light shadows on the dark stairs. She hears music, harsh and disconnected, with someone sobbing lyrics overtop. This is what Stephanie listened to? What she wanted? D could swear she had never heard this music coming from Stephanie's room, only the sugar-sweet pop of all those girls who show their bellies, one indistinguishable from another to D. But then, the door had been closed.

The room below is thick with people. D stands on the last step of the staircase and looks over the crowd. It is like looking at a nest of snakes, writhing in a coiling motion, going nowhere, motivation entirely unfathomable. *I should never, never have come. I should leave now.* Even as she thinks this, her eyes scan the crowd for Stephanie's dark head. She takes the last step down.

Among them D smells sweat, the sweetish acrid scent of pot, alcohol spilled on the dirty floor. She walks blindly through the bodies, wishing she had eaten. The music is making her head hurt and she feels dizzy. The fact that not one of these people has glanced at her, has bumped against her and whirled away without saying a word, makes her feel as if she is disembodied. She sees her feet moving against her will, leading her on this fruitless journey. Then the blond-haired boy is in front of her, his green-haired girl nowhere in sight.

"You came," he says. He looks at her closely. "You look like shit."

He takes her hand and leads her to a dark corridor away from the crowd. It is a bit cooler. The boy leans forward and kisses her. His mouth tastes like smoke; his tongue darts between her lips. For a moment D is motionless, stunned and tired, then she feels his hand on her waist, moving upward and she pushes him away.

"I'm old enough to be your mother."

"No you're not."

"How old are you?"

"Twenty. You would have to be a pretty young mother." He leans forward to kiss her again but

D's head is bent—she searches in her purse for something, something that is always there. He backs away, as if he's thinking of mace, or a tiny siren on a key chain that would cut through the crowd noise and bring security running. D hands him a photograph.

"I'm looking for my daughter."

"Daughter?" The boy takes the photograph and looks at it, his blond hair falling over it.

"I don't know her." He hands it back and says, "We can look around. Lots of street kids here tonight."

D is watching him, she had been willing him to say he knew her, that Stephanie was over there, or there, waiting with his green-haired girlfriend, that Stephanie was a groupie that travelled with the band these past seven months and was behind the stage— high, drunk, but there.

"You need to relax." He is offering her a candy-coloured pill on the palm of his hand. She takes it, swallows it with gin from the bottle he has hidden in his coat. Stupid, she knows, but doesn't care. Stephanie has been taken, not run away. Stolen, snatched, and D knows what that means—she will never see Stephanie again unless they bring her bones to her, the bits of her they find when he is finished with his plaything.

The boy has her hand, is leading her through the crowd. He has taken the photograph from her again and is showing it to people, asking. D watches as they examine the picture, look at her, back down at Stephanie sitting stiffly in the photographer's studio last fall, all her life held in for a proper picture.

D wonders what the hell drug the boy gave her, as things become insignificant, until she almost forgets who is in that photograph the boy keeps handing to people. She dances with the boy maybe, perhaps she sees his green-haired girlfriend kissing another girl next to them; over everything, the pounding music. She meets the band but doesn't remember what she says. Does she show them Stephanie's picture, ask why Stephanie liked this music that seems to have no rhyme or reason? Does she kiss the boy again, are they making love in the alley behind the club among Dumpsters and the sick smell of rancid grease, his blond hair falling over her face like rain? As she comes, the bus shudders to a stop.

The taxi drops her in front of her house. The sky is pearl, pink at its edges. The rain has finally stopped, but the trees still drip slow droplets onto the sidewalk. D fumbles for her keys, drops her purse on the stoop. As she kneels on the wet cement and sweeps the contents back into the bag, she sees that her picture of Stephanie is gone, lost somewhere in the night. She fumbles the door open and leans against it, crying. The phone is ringing in the other room.

Stephanie is home, against the odds. The man who had her—crazy, a cultist who thought he was a god. D cannot believe her fortune. She keeps Stephanie near, and Stephanie seems content to stay close to D. She won't talk about anything that happened while she was with that man. D has learned all she knows from reading Stephanie's statement to the police. She doesn't want to push Stephanie, open wounds. There will be weekly meetings with a psychiatrist for Stephanie, a counsellor for D so that she can handle Stephanie's nightmares and unexpected panic attacks. They will try to pretend Stephanie is still an ordinary teen, but she sees it come down over Stephanie's face like an initiate's opaque veil, even at their happiest times. D knows then that her daughter is back there, in that place she can't follow, the place that mimics death for both of them. The miraculous return is not enough to banish it. Those times Stephanie goes to her room and shuts the door. D stands outside and listens. She hears the music, raucous and indistinct, with lyrics she can never quite make out.

Rites

The wedding had gone perfectly. It was so exciting, just like a wedding in a magazine. She assumed it was a harbinger of what their marriage would be like. She was in love with her handsome husband and he smiled at her. Everyone had told them not to expect much from their honeymoon night, that they would be too tired for much of anything. They were exhausted. When the sun came up the next morning they finally slept.

The light streaming in the windows of their hotel on the sea finally roused them in the late afternoon. She smiled and reached for her husband, who was kneeling on the bed gazing down at her.

"Get up," he said.

"Oh, must we?"

"Yes. Let's go for a walk on the beach."

"So soon, must it start so soon?"

"I don't want to be different than everyone else."

"We won't be."

She had not known this was a worry of his and she was reluctant to go out so soon, but she was happy with him, so she quickly got up. She washed and put on a white linen dress.

"No, not that," he said.

"Why not?"

"You might bleed."

"I bled last night." She showed him the small stain on the sheets. "There won't be any more blood today."

"Just in case," he said.

She nodded, laughing inwardly at his foolishness, feeling very tender toward this man who was hers now. She changed into a short black pleated linen skirt and a light white blouse. Her head rose from the Pierrot collar on the blouse like a bloom, sunny and rosy.

He frowned. "No, no."

Now she was beginning to get a bit upset. "Well, I haven't much different."

He immediately was at her side and stroked her arm. The fine blonde hairs on it rose at his touch.

"I'm sorry, darling. May I pick out what you wear?" He was already heading toward the closet.

A bit sulky, she nodded.

"Darling, to please your husband." His voice was caressing.

He chose a long black dress with high ruffle around the neck and down the front. It was tissue linen so it was not very heavy, but still.

He didn't explain what he meant by wanting her

to wear this, not knowing himself, and she didn't understand. But she dressed without a word and they went out to the beach hand in hand.

On the wide terrace overlooking the beach, with stone steps and balustrades running down, shrubs and trees in closely clipped shapes and red hibiscus, there were throngs of people. They sat at tables drinking pastel-coloured drinks in large frosted glasses, or went up and down the steps with tennis racquets in hand. The women were all dressed as she had been, like school girls in light colours, short skirts and jumpers. She looked younger than all of them, even in the black, with her feet bare and the dress down to mid-calf. She had refused to wear shoes on the beach, and had left her small slippers at the foot of the steps, on a pile of sand. They walked along the beach and began to be happy again. They held hands and watched the great waves rolling in. He wore nothing but shorts, and she admired his tanned torso as the wind whipped her long skirt around her legs.

"Oh, I am so happy. Must we, must we start so soon?" she asked.

"It is part of being married; better to get the beginning over with now, so that we can settle down to life like others."

"I know, my mother told me. I had hoped for a little more time alone."

But she was not really sad, because perhaps they would not start for a long time. Perhaps no one would be interested in them.

"We are alone now, darling," he said, and they looked back at their footsteps on the wet sand.

"May I join you?"

They turned, and there was a man in crumpled white linen. Tall with silver hair. Her husband looked at the man eagerly and she knew that was why he had picked this resort for their honeymoon and not some other, so that things would happen as soon as possible.

"My name is Rex," the tall man said in a low, rather melancholy voice. "Vacation?"

Her husband answered for them: "No, just married."

She crossed her arms over her breasts and looked out to the sea where the sun was setting.

"Newlyweds?"

Her husband, always a man of action, went right to the point. "Which one of us did you come about?"

She could see how truly anxious he was for this married life to begin.

"I thought we might talk a bit," the man said.

For the first time she looked straight at Rex and

their eyes met. She knew it was her he had come about. Before any more could be said, though, people began to gather at the foot of the stone terrace with their drinks. Someone was splashing in the water, laughing. A woman came dripping out of the waves. She wore a short white bathing dress, which clung to her heavy curves. Her white-gold hair was slicked off her forehead, and she walked out of the sea on heavily muscled, tanned legs. The girl knew this was a Queen.

In a rich, booming voice, the woman called out to them, "My girlfriend is going to have a child with her husband, my last boyfriend has a new job, my mother-in-law has a new lover at the age of seventy-seven; where else but in our society could this be? Everyone is happy and no one is fighting, no one is jealous."

The crowd laughed and clapped. Only Rex, her husband and she stood silent. Her husband was silent because he was in thrall to this creature. The girl saw that and it made her despair. The Queen had also noticed her husband standing silently on the beach and was looking right at him.

"Come on, darling," she said. "Let's go. I'll show this boy how hard I like it."

The crowd laughed again. No preliminaries for the Queen, no talking. Straightforward, just like her husband. Two porters ran down the balustrade steps with trays of pastries in hand. The Queen grabbed an éclair and took a bite, her strong white teeth severing it neatly in two. The other half she handed to the girl's husband and wrapped her arm around his waist while he ate it. He could not take his eyes off the woman, and looked, she thought, like a boy seeing his first Christmas tree. His cheeks were flushed and he willingly followed the Queen up the stone steps to the wide terrace, where waiters had lit small lamps on the tables so that all the people's faces flickered and lost shape. She and Rex followed behind. She was not able to let her husband go yet; Rex followed because, well, only Rex knew why he was still following. On the terrace the woman was wrapped in her furs and with shining eyes stood in the doorway of the hotel, holding out her hand to the girl's husband, who was moving toward her.

Look hard now, the girl thought, *look hard. After this, everything changes. See the way the light comes through the lace curtains in the hotel windows and falls on your husband's face, see the woman in the doorway flanked by men and the great torches burning there in the iron holders. She is magnificent. Who is it that chooses the hunters and the hunted?*

She and Rex stood in the dark outside of the torches' light and watched her husband go into the hotel with the Queen and her retinue.

The girl ran down the stone steps into the

dark, wanting to be alone, but she knew Rex was still behind her. She had not thought it would be like this—she had seen it as she and her husband together, then a small break, and then they would be back together again, a neat diagram. But here was Rex, and that woman, and after them another and another, and no one minded.

"Didn't your mother tell you?" It was Rex's voice beside her in the dark.

"Yes. But she said when it first happened to her it was cats dancing and sunny and a lovely time."

"For some people it is like that, for others it is the other side. The dark knight card, the black night of it."

Then Rex leaned over and kissed her, bending her like a green branch and she knew there was nothing for it but to submit.

Peach Festival

Alexis and her little brother sat at the breakfast table and tried to ignore the rising voices, the hectoring tone of the words spilling out of their parents in the next room. They pushed brightly coloured cold cereal around in their bowls, the sweetish, slightly sour smell making Alexis gag a little. Usually they had pancakes on Saturday morning, but their parents had started early today, and Alexis had been in charge of filling her and Scott's bowls, pouring the juice in the plastic juice cups while the argument went on in the other room. The bright red kitchen cupboards shone like polished fairytale apples in the morning sun; it would be a great day for the Peach Festival, if they ever got there. Finally, the voices fell silent. Alexis heard her father pound up the stairs, and the slam of the upstairs bathroom door. Her mother came in the kitchen a few minutes later, cheeks flushed, mouth slightly open. Alexis could see the wet gleam of her mother's teeth through her parted lips, and looked away, back down into her cereal bowl, where amorphously shaped pastel marshmallows were turning the water a sickly pink.

"You kids got breakfast? Good, here's the money, Alexis, half for you, half for Scotty. I'll drop you guys off and pick you up at six by the entrance, no fooling around. Keep your cells on. I think at fifteen you should be able to handle this, right, Lexy? You are in absolute charge of your brother. You hear that, Scotty? I am in no mood for fairs today. I've got to run some errands, but I will be back at six, no later. Now let's get out of here before that asshole comes back down."

Alexis's mother grabbed her purse off the counter and hustled the kids out the door. Their cereal bowls remained on the table, the contents dissolving into an inedible, sodden mess.

The Ferris wheel hung over the fairgrounds like a skeletal sun. With every drop it made, there were screams and laughter, which floated over the grounds to where Alexis and Scott stood waiting in line for tickets. Alexis was on her cell—her friends were already deep inside the fair, beyond the metal ticket booths and turnstiles, enjoying the promises of excitement that Scott and Alexis could just make out over the shoulders of people in front of them as they stood in line.

"Let's meet . . . two please." Alexis paid for the tickets without taking the phone away from her ear. She handed one to Scott and pushed through the turnstile. "I'm in," she told her friends on the other end of the phone. "Let's meet here—" Her eyes swept the area just inside the ticket booth. "—by this metal pole, with the picture of the missing girl on it. Hurry, I can't wait to see what's up; my parents were such jerk-offs this morning, I swear I thought I'd never get here. Hurry."

She clicked the phone shut and leaned against the silver pole, her eyes scanned the crowd for any signs of her friends.

"Lexy, can I have my money?"

She looked down at her brother. "Weren't you supposed to meet Tim or Jim or one of your friends or something?"

"Yeah, we're meeting in the agricultural building."

Alexis made a face. "That place smells like shit."

"Shut up, Lexy. Give me my money."

"Don't you want to call them or something?"

"No, I don't want to call them, I want to go over and find them. They were going to be in the building. It's not that big, I'll find them."

Alexis looked at her brother's open freckled face, with the little nick on one cheek that looked like an insect had taken a bite of his pink skin. Hanging out with him all day would drive her nuts anyway.

"Fine. Here's your half, but be back here at six sharp. Mom would kill me if she knew I was letting you run off. *I'll* kill you if you're late, you little jerk."

"I'm eleven, I think I can handle the frickin' Peach Festival."

They both laughed and Scott walked away, into the crowds that came together and parted over and over.

Alexis leaned against the pole and flipped open her phone. She scanned back text messages, and changed the screen to read Sexy Lexy, and called her voice mail even though she knew no one had called her since she last checked. While she was listening to the tinny voice telling her nothing in chillingly polite tones, someone grabbed her arm.

"Lexy, always on the phone. Calling one of your boyfriends?"

Alexis shut the phone and dropped it in her purse.

"Jesus, Tiffany, you nearly gave me a heart attack."

Tiffany swung her long red hair over her shoulder and grinned. "You are such a spaz. Me and Erin have been looking for you for hours."

Erin, who was on the phone, waggled her fingers at them, her blonde bob swinging over the receiver as she whispered something into it, then clicked the phone shut. Alexis turned away impatiently. Erin really did have someone to talk to on the phone. She met guys on the Internet, in teen chat rooms, and they always called her. Boys from their class at school called Erin too, ostensibly to talk about assignments or some other school activity, but really just to sit in silence, happy to listen while Erin went on about her friends, her teachers, anything she felt like talking about.

"God, look at that ugly bitch. Who would kidnap her?" Erin was standing staring up at the poster of the missing girl.

"Erin," Tiffany laughed, "you are so bold."

"Well, you'd have to be pretty stupid in this day and age to let anyone kidnap you."

"I think she goes to our school," Alexis said. The picture was hard to make out, the pixels blurring the face into anonymity, but something about it seemed familiar.

There was no name on the poster, which seemed weird, just a phone number and the words: "Have you seen this girl?"

"Oh great, I'm sure we'll hear all about it when we get back to school. Who cares? There are absolutely no cute guys here. Let's go on some rides before I die of boredom." Erin led them toward the midway, Tiffany and Alexis on either side of her, their arms locked together in a soft linkage of tan young limbs, fuzzed with sun-lightened hairs, like the skin of a peach.

❦

Scott stood outside the archway to the agricultural building. They had set up a cut-out of a giant wooden peach at the entrance. It wasn't the hottest paint job in the world, but Scott thought it had managed to catch something of the freshness of peaches, how that colour on the outside advertised the sweetness of the first bite. Wasn't there some book he had had to read for school about a kid who had lived in a giant peach? With bugs for friends? The kid had seemed like a dope to Scott, kind of whiny, but he didn't remember much else about the book.

He went into the agricultural building, which was made of stone with high vaulted ceilings. The air was a lot cooler than outside and it smelled of animals. Grassy, dark and warm under the circulating currents of cool air. He looked at the cows and stopped to see the prize-winning peach pie display. Some ugly quilts, some pigs. Pigs always looked to Scott as if they knew some secret, as if they were laughing at him, smiles on their snouts, half-closed eyes. He had hated the story of the three pigs as a child and wished he could rewrite it so the wolf ate them up right away, before they started their building and breaking and killing.

He wandered over to the area of the building where the prize chickens were being displayed. Without thinking, he flipped open his phone and dialled Tim, who was supposed to meet him here, near the chickens. *No Service*. In the stone building Scott couldn't get any bars at all on his phone. Shit, he'd have to go outside and try from there. Or he could just go into the chicken area and look around. Tim was probably right inside staring at some rooster or something. Scott put his phone in his back pocket and stepped through the doorway that led deeper into the agricultural building.

The three girls had been up and down the midway once already. They had bought cotton candy, which tasted like the sugar cereal Alexis had for breakfast. They unwrapped the long sugary pink strands with their fingers, which they sucked clean as they walked.

Carnies called to them in voices that carried over the noise of the crowds: *Hey cutie, come on and play, I'll make it worth your while; Sweetheart, I've got three balls for you, I'll throw in an extra one for free; Lookit that, three peaches, how 'bout if I play the game and you girls be the prize.*

A tall man wearing a soiled jean jacket, with long hair that swung in his face, staggered up to them. He leaned into Alexis and said, "Smile, sunshine, it can't be that bad." The three girls skittered away, giggling, Erin and Tiffany laughing about Lexy's new boyfriend, but Alexis felt he was still watching her. She turned her head quickly to look over her shoulder, but the crowd was thick and she couldn't see him if he was there, only the carnies leaning on their booths while their calls endlessly rose above the mass of people crawling along the midway.

The smell hit Scott right away. He had to agree with his sister; the place did smell like shit. He hadn't known chickens were so stinky. Heavy wire cages piled on top of tables held more varieties of chickens than Scott had ever realized existed. There were deep green iridescent feathers, rust-coloured feathers, plumes nodding on heads, bald heads showing pimply skin, chickens with strange mop-tops that hung in their eyes so they looked like the Beatles, all of them clucking and gabbling. Occasionally the cry of a rooster would punctuate the mayhem. The sound, familiar to Scott only from movies or cartoons, made him shiver and tense his shoulders, waiting for the unpredictable next cry.

Scott could tell the roosters were angry, too many other roosters in their space; they wanted to kick the shit out of somebody. He looked at the caged birds, their naked and hard feet with curved nails, each mean beak set in a sharp point that would stab to get what it wanted. He opened his phone again, but there was still no service. He was giving up on Tim; he had to get out of this stink. He would try him from outside and if he got a hold of him, great—if not, well, he would go on some rides and then call Lexy to meet him.

He started walking back toward the entrance to the main agricultural building when a rooster in one of the cages started to crow. It was all white feathers, with elaborate plumes falling over its face. Its beak was reddish pink, opened now in a piercing cry. Scott took a step closer and the bird stopped. It shuffled in its cage and the feathers over its face moved side to side. He saw its inhuman, avian eye looking past him, cold and determined, and when it shook its head again and the feathers shifted and settled, he saw its other eye was nothing more than an empty red socket with white foam oozing over its rim.

The three girls decided to go on the Himalaya first. They stood in line and gossiped and Erin got another call on her phone. It was a boy from their class, and all three girls took turns talking to him. The metallic rattle of the ride, the linked cars speeding around on the lifting and falling track punctuated their conversation. When they made it to the front of the line, the three girls grabbed for a car, but the carnie running the ride stopped them.

"Sorry gals, only two to a car."

"What? You're kidding." Erin swung her blonde hair out of her face and put her hands on her hips. "We want to ride together."

"Them's the rules. You and red get in this car, and I'll put your friend right behind you."

"God, what a rip. Okay, come on, Tiff." Erin grabbed Tiffany's hand and climbed into the car, pulling the bar over their legs.

"Sorry, Lexy," Tiffany said, and then she turned to Erin who was waving at three boys in another car.

The carnie took Alexis by the arm and sat her two cars behind Tiffany and Erin.

"Hey, there were three boys in that car, how come . . . ?" But the carnie brought the bar down hard across Alexis's thighs before she could finish.

"You're just a little too plump to squeeze in there with your girlfriends." The carnie ran a hand across her thigh. "I like your jeans, where'd you get those jeans?"

Alexis's cheeks were burning. "My father bought them for me."

"My father's dead." He took his hand off her thigh and grinned.

The ride started with a jerk. The cars spun around the track, while rock music from twenty years ago played loudly.

The carnie called over the loudspeaker, "Do you wanna go faster?"

Everyone on the ride screamed "yes" except Alexis. Tears were running down her face and being whipped away by the speed of the ride.

She saw Erin's hands go up into the air in front of her, and the carnie called, "Do you wanna go backwards?"

Again the screams, and Alexis slid to one side of the car and couldn't move, the ride's force keeping her against the side of the car, the skin on her cheeks stinging as the tears dried and the wind pulled them taut. A high-pitched siren started and the ride went even faster. The fairgrounds were a blur—the other people in the cars in front of her seemed to melt into one stream of colour and noise. Alexis put her head down and waited for the ride to stop.

"Another chicken got him."

Scott turned to see who was speaking to him. It was an older boy in a black Nirvana t-shirt. He was probably Lexy's age, Scott thought.

"Is it yours?" Scott asked.

"Hell no, I just saw them separate the two birds this morning after one put this one's eye out. They probably would have killed each other."

Scott and the boy looked at the bird in silence. It strutted around its cage in baleful silence, fixing them alternately with its good eye and the foaming hole.

"Actually, I'm with the sideshows. Well, my mother is. We travel with the midway."

Scott looked at the boy with new interest. Wait

till he told Tim he met a carnie, or at least a carnie's kid.

"Cool. What's your mom do? Does she run a ride?"

"She's Madame Leyenska, the fortune teller." The boy spat into the dirt. "Let's get out of here, this place stinks."

Scott and the boy walked back out onto the fairgrounds. Scott checked his phone and saw that the battery was dead. He had forgotten to plug it in last night. This day was turning out to be a bust. For a minute he'd hoped this carnie kid could maybe get him on his mom's ride, but his mother was some freaky fortune teller.

"Well, it was nice meeting you." Scott stuck his phone back in his pocket. "But I'm supposed to be meeting a friend around here, and I should try to find him." He looked into the crowds milling around the agricultural building, hoping to see Tim.

"Hey, don't you want my mom to tell your fortune?" The boy grabbed Scott's t-shirt from the back.

"No. I don't believe in that crap. Let go, I've gotta find my sister."

The boy dropped his hand and Scott shrugged his shoulder under the shirt to get the feeling of the boy's sweaty palm off of him. The boy stuck his hands in his pockets and spat again. "Whatever, just thought you'd want to know if your parents were getting divorced." The boy started to walk away.

Scott stood there for a minute, fingers pressed against his useless phone, and then went after him.

The ride ended and Alexis staggered off. She didn't see the carnie, or Erin and Tiffany, and she didn't care. She sat down on a bench and put her head between her knees.

"Oh, Alexis, you are such a wuss."

She could smell Erin's sugary perfume.

"Hey, are you okay?" Tiffany sat down next to her.

"Yeah, just needed to catch my breath." Alexis raised her head. Erin was a short way away, talking on her cell.

"God, that ride was so fun. We're going on the Tilt-a-Whirl next. Wanna come?"

"No, you two go. I'll wait here on this bench; maybe I'll get some water."

Tiffany looked at Alexis closely. "Well, if you're sure." Erin waved to them from over by the ride. "Okay, well I'll tell Erin. We'll meet you back here, okay?"

Alexis just nodded, closed her eyes and put her head down again. When she looked up, the girls were gone and she was alone.

Anyone who saw the two boys walking together would have taken them for brothers. Both skinny, wearing black t-shirts and baseball caps; the younger, shorter of the two was maybe ten or eleven, the older fourteen or so. They walked close to each other, bumping shoulders but they didn't hold hands. That would be beneath their dignity, no matter what their parents might have told them about keeping close in the chaos of the fairground, the older responsible for the safety of the younger. The two of them entered a small grouping of tents and trailers, away from the main thrust of the fair, where there were no crowds of jostling teens and haggard-looking parents toting younger children. The older boy looked around quickly, and then, taking the younger boy by the hand, pulled him between the flaps of a nondescript grey tent.

The yellow lights of the midway were coming on. From her position outside of the fairgrounds, in the field behind the trailers and tents, Alexis watched them glow like fireflies caught in a jar. The ground beneath her back smelled of crushed grass, the end of summer. From the peach orchards nearby came the scent of fallen fruit, mangled, sweet and sickly. The phone in her hand began to ring, and was flung far into the tall grass where it would go unanswered until its battery finally went dead. She didn't brush away the insect that settled on the curve of her cheek, its slender proboscis quivering through the fine hairs, tasting.

In the Grass

The birds woke him up. Their calls disturbed the velvet of his sleep in such a way that, for a moment, it seemed he understood their song.

Too deep, too deep, they repeated, until finally the words dissolved back into chaos of meaningless notes.

Without opening his eyes, he turned and reached for her, but instead of the soft skin of her shoulder, he felt the boar bristle of dried grass beneath his fingers. Startled, he sat up. The expected crumple of floral sheets and duvet was now a circle of burnt and broken stalks, with a low mound at its centre. She was gone.

Long grasses that waved and sighed surrounded the flattened circle where he had been lying. He stood on the mound to get his bearings, to look for her. As far as he could see, there was nothing but undulating green. The sun was directly overhead in a blank and blue sky. What scout lore he knew—moss on the north side of the tree, direction told from the position of the sun—was useless.

He shouted her name over and over, but only the birds answered, invisible in the unbroken expanse.

Just at the edge of his vision, there on the horizon, the tall blades parted and closed with a shiver, as if something moved among them, close to the ground.

Was it her? Should he make his way through and try to meet her? But if he left and lost his way, and she came to meet him here—

There was another ripple, perhaps moving in his direction, perhaps not. It might only have been the wind.

He sat down in the burnt circle to wait.

He fell asleep and dreamt of birds, their eyes like ball bearings set in carved sockets, unseeing. Their tiny claws curled like steel hasps around stems that bowed low beneath their weight. From shining scarlet beaks the birds sang her name with mechanical repetition.

When he woke again, it was dark. A full moon rose, emerald and low, like a lidless eye turned on him.

Using his hands, he began to tear clumps of burnt stubble away from the mounded earth, digging down through the clotted dirt. Not far beneath the surface, his fingers caught in a tangle of hair like the fine roots of grass.

Close behind, the grasses rustled.

The Other Side

Hilario stood on the path to the side door. Even in the dying light she could tell it was him from the size. At six foot six, Hilario was hard to mistake for anyone else in the neighbourhood. Maddy stopped on the sidewalk up to her house, her dark hair spilling over the collar of her plaid fall coat, her fists jammed deep in her pockets against the chill in the air. The pretty suburban street that her house was on was empty, everyone in for supper or television. Curtains pulled against the creeping night. Or maybe they were drawn against what they knew was coming. The street had witnessed too many fights between Hilario and his wife, Caroline. There had been too many times when Maddy or one of the other neighbours had had to call the police, the flashing red and blue lights out of place among the manicured lawns and seasonal flags.

Maddy was not going to let that man keep her from her home. Alex was in there, asleep in bed, waiting for the medicine she had run to the drugstore to get him. She had hated to leave him alone—even ten seemed too young to Maddy to be in an empty house, but with her husband Andrew gone for the week, she had had no choice. His fever was high, a schoolyard cold, but still, children's Tylenol was needed or else he wouldn't be able to sleep through the night. And now Hilario hulked on her walk, illuminated only by the motion detector light from the side porch. It threw a long beam despite the lilac bushes banked on either side of the door.

She only had the side-door key with her. They never used the front door. It opened onto a cramped foyer, with a closet stuffed with old hats, skates and household detritus. The side door opened onto the laundry room just off the kitchen. Resolutely Maddy walked up the path where Hilario waited. He stepped aside to let her pass, but grabbed her arm. Although his fingers lightly encircled her forearm, Maddy could feel the power there, knew that if he tightened his grip he could snap the bone.

"Hilario, let me go," she said, twisting her wrist against his hold.

"Maddy, where are Caroline and Joseph?"

"I know what happened," Maddy said, her voice strong. "They finally left, didn't they?"

Caroline was Maddy's best friend. Maddy could see her in her mind's eye, thin face pale with worry, lilac shadows beneath her eyes, the beautiful red hair pulled back in a ponytail that fell halfway down her back. Caroline's son Joseph, the same age as Alex, had Caroline's red hair and Hilario's dark eyes, but was pale too, and trembled, and wouldn't speak to Maddy when she spoke to him. How many times had they spent the night in this house, trying to escape Hilario? Now they had finally left. Gone to relatives or to the police or a halfway house, Maddy didn't know. She hadn't spoken to Caroline for two days; but she was glad she had finally gone, and taken Joseph with her.

"Maddy, where is Joseph?" Hilario's grip on her arm tightened.

"Let me go or I'll scream." She wrenched her arm away from Hilario and ran up the path to her door. She felt his weight behind her, but she made it to the door first and had it opened when he grabbed her arm again.

"Maddy, what has she done with Joseph?"

"Hilario, if you lay a hand on me once more, I'll call the police." She and Hilario stood on the little porch outside the door; in the yellow light from the overhead fixture his face was distorted. He might have been drinking, there was a faint smell of alcohol, and even at five nine, Maddy would be no match for Hilario if he decided to get rough. Maddy damned the high lilac bushes that hid the little side porch from the neighbours.

"I'll scream, Hilario, I'll scream so loud, the whole neighbourhood will come running."

Hilario dropped her arm, but as she went in the door he grabbed the handle from behind and started to pull against her. They struggled each on either side of the door, but Maddy had the door almost closed before he grabbed it so she had the advantage. She almost had it shut when a strangled yowl made her look down. A small paw and the nose of her lilac point Siamese cat, Zara, were stuck in the crack. Maddy considered slamming the door shut anyway, but the thought of Zara's paw being mangled or her being left out there with Hilario in the state he was in frightened her more than his getting in the door. Hilario had never hit her, only threatened her. It was Caroline's stories about what Hilario did, that gave her cold ripples in her stomach. Those stories had sometimes remained with her for weeks, turning up in her nightmares. Maddy would wake up crying and Andrew would hold her until she fell back to sleep. She eased up a little on the door and Zara brushed against her ankles as she ran in. There was no longer any resistance on the other side of the door. Hilario was gone.

Maddy pulled the door shut firmly and locked it. She felt in the pocket of her plaid coat for the pharmacy paper bag, but it was gone. It must have fallen out on the path when she was fighting with Hilario. Well, she was not going back out there tonight. Alex would have to have half an adult Tylenol with some juice. He would complain about the taste, but it was what he needed. Those children with their unwashed hands, sharing candies and colds in equal measures, like little animals.

Maddy hung up her coat, and stepped out of the hospital scrubs she was wearing. She hadn't even changed after coming off her shift at the hospital before running to the store. She saw with distaste that there were smears of blood on the top. Maddy threw them in the washer. She put on the heavy chenille robe hanging from a hook in the laundry room.

After she had started the washer, she walked into the kitchen. It was her favourite room in the house. Painted lilac and green, there were framed pieces of Alex's artwork on the walls and an old blue wooden table and chairs she had painted herself. She thought of all the times she and Caroline had sat at that table and had coffee, while Joseph had coloured with Alex's crayons at the other side. She had listened to her stories about Hilario, his looming shadow always hovering over Caroline's shoulder, even when he was miles away. Maddy had urged her to leave again and again. Now Caroline had finally done it and Maddy hoped she and Joseph were safe, wherever they were.

The house was quiet. Alex must still be asleep. Maddy went to the refrigerator and got out the apple juice and poured it into a glass grabbed from the dish drainer. She turned to go into the living room and saw that the slatted folding doors between the two rooms were partially shut. Maddy stood still, the juice glass gripped in her hand. Behind her, the kitchen clock clicked steadily. She knew she had left the doors open when she went out to the store. Through the crack of the doors she could see the light on in the living room, and Hilario's shadow. How had he gotten in? The only other way was through the front door and there was no way he would have a key to that. Andrew had one on his key ring, and there was one in the living room in an old ceramic bowl, but Hilario wouldn't have had either. He must have broken a window somewhere. She heard his voice murmuring, as if he was on the telephone with someone.

"I can't upset her . . . she'll never tell if she thinks . . . Yes, I'll go slowly."

Maddy couldn't catch the rest of what he was saying.

She looked around the kitchen for a weapon. She put the glass back on the counter and went to the laundry room. It couldn't be a knife. Maddy hated knives, was afraid to handle them. Caroline had always laughed at her for this, had been the one to slice the limes for their gin and tonics, or the lemons for the boys' lemonade. In the laundry room, she picked up Alex's bat that was leaning in the corner, under the hook for his coat. Maddy felt weak. Hilario was between her and her son. Alex's Yankees baseball cap was on a shelf above the hooks. She felt a thrum of fear go through her. She took the bat in both hands and moved back through the kitchen. She paused outside the door again. A framed picture of a crayon drawing of a boy and a cat hung next to the doorframe. It was signed Joseph. Maddy smiled and hefted the bat higher.

For Caroline and Joseph.

She pushed open the door and ran into the living room, hoping to catch Hilario off guard.

Her first swing caught him in the stomach and he grunted in surprise, but he was ready for her next swing and caught the bat easily in his hands.

"Maddy," he said. He pulled at the bat; she began to pull too, her hair swinging wildly around her face.

"Let me go, let me go."

"Maddy," his voice was low and careful, "where is Joseph?"

Maddy let go of the bat and backed away from Hilario, toward the fireplace.

"I don't know. I haven't talked to Caroline for two days. I don't know where Caroline and Joseph have gone." Her back was against the fireplace now. To her left the stairs that lead to the second floor went up into darkness. She had forgotten to leave the light on for Alex. Thank God the noise had not woken him up. Maddy didn't want to scream and have him stumble down here into something frightening.

"Hilario, just get out."

"Maddy, I need to know where Joseph is." He advanced toward her, his hands out as if in supplication.

"Oh, Hilario." Maddy shook her head. "Do you think I would tell you even if I knew? I know all about you. I heard all the stories from Caroline. Everyone thinks you're such a good man, a pillar of the community, but they know the truth on this block, don't they? Her father told her not to marry a dirty Mexican, but even he didn't know how evil you are. How you would try to convince the doctors she was crazy. Make her take handfuls of pills that made her sleep all day so you could have other women over. She found their things in her bedroom, Hilario; did you think she wouldn't notice? How you tried to take Joseph to live with your parents in Mexico, but the judge put a stop to that, didn't he? How you hit her and beat her and made her eat dirt and lick the floors and cut herself and—"

"Maddy, Maddy." Hilario was trying to grab a hold of her.

Maddy's voice rose to a hysterical pitch; she

slid down the fireplace to sit on the floor. She was laughing as tears coursed down her cheeks.

"And you and Joseph had secrets and I knew you were talking about me and I knew you put things in my food and he would be walking around the halls at night with a knife coming to get me."

She pulled at her face, her red hair completely out of its band looking like tongues of fire licking at her cheeks.

"Caroline," Hilario was almost whispering, kneeling in front of her. "Is that you, are you here? Do you remember you were at the hospital?"

"I work there, I work there," Caroline's voice rose to a screech. "I work in that clean hospital where there are no germs, no dirt, no, no, no, no!"

Hilario shook her, his hands tight on her arms.

"You left the hospital, Caroline, you picked Joseph up from school. He wasn't there when I went to get him, where is he?"

"He had a fever, he was sick from all the germs, from all your dirt."

"Goddamn it, Caroline, where is he?" For the first time Hilario raised his voice.

Upstairs they heard a scratching and low plaintive calls. It was Zara, Joseph's cat clawing at a door upstairs. Hilario pushed Caroline aside roughly and took the stairs two at a time. He stopped in front of his son's bedroom door. Zara was clawing frantically at it. Hilario saw the bloody prints on the doorknob and began to cry. He pushed opened the door. Joseph's bed was a gory mess, the sheets were torn apart, soaked red. Zara followed Hilario in and the heavy metallic tang of the blood drove her out again to huddle mewling in the bathtub, clawing at the sides frantically. A silver scalpel lay amongst the mess on the sheets, but his son wasn't there.

Caroline's voice floated up from the bottom of the stairs, reasonable, triumphant.

"I sterilized it first, Hilario, I sterilized it first."

Hilario picked up the scalpel.

Dr. Johnson's Daughter

The scientists are at the mounds as always. The light is getting low in the sky but the scientists are still at work. Back and forth silently in white coats, the assistants follow behind them like courtiers, clipboards in hand, to catch their every word, every notion. Voices are pitched low, so that there seems to be a soft hum as a constant counterpoint to the movement around the mounds. Against the skyline, pieces of equipment stand ready. Huge machines with radar panels of open mesh, silhouetted as the sun dips below the horizon. The lamps come on and cast a blue glow from their halogen bulbs, circles of light punctuated by dark spaces, so that to walk between them is like falling into a pit, only to be lifted back out into the familiar at the next lamp. Dr. Johnson is among the scientists. His tall, white-haired form moves among the others, gives directions, bends over his colleagues' work. His eyes are so hooded that he appears to be half asleep as he walks, but he is not. He is watching.

In the dormitories, Dr. Johnson's daughter Erena
plays a game of basketball on the indoor court. She
too is tall, with long brown hair caught in a ponytail
that whips her shoulders as she turns and feints
in the moves of the game. A feeling of absolute
competence suffuses her on the court, any type
of court—like the feeling she gets at a computer,
feeding in calculations and computations, deciding
the best way to disseminate numeric information
so that it is accessible to all the scientists, not just
her brilliant father and the few others of his stature.
Erena's eyes are round, almost as if a cartoonist has
drawn them. They are wide open and unblinking in
their innocence. She does not question much, but
like an animal, she rejoices in what she is given.

In a brightly lit Quonset hut, the scientists have
gathered for the day's debriefing. Dr. Johnson is
figuring something in his head. He asks the scientists
to come back out with him to the mounds. Though
most of them are ready for bed, maybe a drink in the
canteen, they follow him out.

The mounds themselves are of baked greyish-
red earth, in a pyramidal form. They are very long,
running hundreds of metres in one direction. They
are about eight feet tall, though the measurements
vary slightly from mound to mound. Both slat sides
of the mound are covered with slight ridges, no more

than an inch or so long, which are arranged into columns.

No one knows what the mounds are for. There is a feeling, shared widely by the scientific community and the government, that they are very important and must be studied. That is why fifteen years ago this outpost was set up. They have been told to take it very slow. To do no drilling until all surface features of the mounds have been recorded, soil samples taken and retaken, the ground around them sifted for relics or indications of what they might be. The scientists are beginning to get a bit impatient, though none of them will say so. They don't understand why the mounds cannot just be drilled into after all these years—they are obviously the tombs of some aboriginal society and really this is work for the archaeologists.

No one talks about the strange things that happen here. If someone has had an incident, they keep it to themselves; join in the rumblings of discontent. None of the scientists really want to leave anyway as this is a cushy job, with more perks than anything the outside world can offer.

Erena Johnson is surrounded by friends when she comes off the court and heads to the showers.

"Come for coffee."

"Come to the lounge to listen to music."

"Can you come to my room later?"

They clamour for her attention.

These dormitories are where the students stay. They are here to learn the job of examining the mounds. Competition for positions is fierce and it is a great honour to be chosen. Some of the older students have already been out around the mounds, have been assigned to assist a certain scientist. When their schooling is finished, they will move into the family compound and become full-fledged assistants and, someday, scientists themselves.

Dr. Johnson lives in the family compound alone. Erena's mother is dead. He and Erena have supper together almost every night. On the weekends, they walk among the pine trees that hide the dormitories and compound and surround the clearing the mounds are in. Some of the trees are thousands of years old. They tower over the buildings, jagged spikes on their trunks until they spread into the sparse branches tipped with green needles. Smaller trees are fuller and softer, their greenness feathery to the touch. Erena has walked among these trees since she was a toddler. Sometimes Dr. Johnson will take Erena to the mounds. No one is supposed to go near them unless specially authorized and in an official capacity, but Dr. Johnson is so high-ranking, he is never questioned.

❧

Dr. Johnson has the scientists out by the mounds. He stands in the light facing the mounds, while the others stand in a semi-circle facing him, waiting with curiosity to see what Johnson has to say that couldn't wait until the morning. The light halos his head as he begins to explain.

"It's the markings. We have been working on the assumption that they are anything from binary code to hieroglyphics, to mere decoration, but it's like that awful book that Erena had as a child—that magic eye, senseless patterns until you look just the right way and then Mickey Mouse or something. If you look just the right way—"

Dr. Johnson turns his head. Again, like today while he was examining them, the markings shift; they blur, and then begin to settle into the message. A sweep of bright lights in front of him breaks his view. It is a Jeep, a government Jeep. The other scientists who had been turning to look at the mound, to see what Dr. Johnson saw, blink in its light.

A beefy man in a blue suit gets out.

"Gentlemen, may I ask that you return to the Meeting Area. Very important information has come to light."

Dr. Johnson blinks and shakes his head; he almost had it, what could be more important than that? But he will be able to look again in the morning. He'll have his assistant ready to write down exactly what he sees. With the other scientists he returns to the hut where the man in blue is waiting.

Erena comes out of the shower. She is wearing a white tank top and men's boxers, roughly towelling her hair dry. As she steps into her room, she hears voices in the corridor. She opens the door.

"That's it then, they've fired the whole lot of them."

"Budget cuts, I hear."

"Too close to the project, they need fresh blood."

One of Erena's friends sees her standing in the doorway.

"Oh Erena, they've fired all the top scientists on the project. They have to be out by tomorrow."

Her friend comes and puts an arm around her. "I'm sure they'll let you stay on, you're one of the best students."

Erena looks at him with her wide, round eyes. "I wouldn't want to. I better go pack."

He drops his arm. "Erena, come for coffee in the lounge when you're through, won't you?"

Erena nods *yes*, and closes her door. In her room, she pulls out a suitcase and throws it on the bed. Not much to pack, some white t-shirts, a sweater or two, the black dress she wears for important dinners.

Underwear. She moves back and forth from the dresser to the bed with her small piles of clothing over and over until the dresser is empty. She stands as if awaiting orders, what to do next. Where is her father? She looks down at her feet, at the rug. It has a pattern of abstract red roses with twining blue stems. The same rug as in all the dorms, and in her father's room in the family compound.

As she looks, the stems begin to writhe, twisting. Blue ink is spilling across them. Did she spill it while writing a paper? But it is resolving itself, resolving itself into something she needs to know.

She is interrupted by running feet in the hall, loud voices.

"They're moving them out tonight. What the hell—"

Erena sees lights outside her window, the sound of transport engines. She opens the doors to her balcony and steps out.

Next to her the tall pines stretch upward and far below she sees the convoy. Her father is there somewhere. He is being taken away.

Dr. Johnson has been rushed out. He was not given time to pack his things. They will be packed for him and sent on from the compound. His daughter will be notified and sent to join him later. A vague, important new job is the reason for this immediate departure with his fellow scientists, all those who were out there with him at the mounds. He is hustled into an open Jeep. He stands up as they pass the dormitories. The convoy, too big for the narrow access road into the area, has slowed to a halt. Dr. Johnson looks up, searching. He sees Erena on her balcony.

Erena, too, sees her father.

She begins to wave, frantic.

"Wait for me, wait for me, Daddy."

Then she pitches over the balcony edge.

Erena falls past the pines in slow motion. She is not afraid. If she dies she will merely be dead and will not know what happened. She seems to be wrapped in light, dim yellow light.

If her father's science is right, she will land beside him; if the message is what she thinks it might be. But for now she has no way of knowing, and can only see herself falling spread-eagled past the endless pines, while the lights of the convoy move farther away.

While He Sleeps

I hover above his face. See the slight bulge and roll of his eye beneath closed lids as he dreams something I can't see. I slip beneath the lids over the moist convexity of his eye's surface. Behind the lid it is blue-black with faint veins, lightning on a clear night sky. I want to imprint myself on his retina, enter his dream. Instead, I slide further down under his skin and, for a moment, I have form. I can't stay long there. His being pushes me out. I stroke him with my tongue as I float away.

Tonight there is another one beside him. She watches the dark with wide-open eyes, blankets pulled to her chin. I trail my fingers across her hair to let her know I watch, and in the dark she starts and turns to him, buries her head in his back. I watch through the one-way mirror of death.

There is no hierarchy of souls as promised us by the Sunday school teachers, there is no children's illustrated Bible with golden-haired angels bending over a cradle. I am alone here.

This morning the other one is still in the house. She stays while he is at work. Trailing about the rooms draped in an afghan, with a mug cupped in her hands. I follow her. She pauses in front of the photographs on the mantelpiece, rights one that has fallen over. She peers closely at them, touches each face with her fingertip.

How long she has been here, I don't know; all days run into one. I only know that she has been here too long, that the air is changed, and her scent is beginning to obliterate mine. My scent, the scent of dark roses, tipped with thorns, arranged in a cut glass vase on a table somewhere.

I can't follow him into the world, escape her slow absorption of me. I am bounded by the square of this place, slick walls with no handhold. She never goes out either. Only sleeps, or sits on the sofa, like some favoured concubine awaiting her master's pleasure. I laugh in her ear, taunt her passivity and she turns her head, a dog hearing a sound humans can't hear.

In the late afternoons, she takes a long bath in the claw-footed tub. Readies herself for him. Caresses herself with the washcloth: breasts, thighs. She imagines he is touching her. Her thoughts are strong. They run before me, a movie in a dank theatre smelling of men making furtive motions in the dark.

Through her mind's eye I see them arrive

separately at a restaurant. In the hall between the kitchen and the bathrooms he pushes her against a wall, thrusts a hand under her skirt while platters clatter beside them. Only the voice of an approaching waiter sends them apart, faces flushed, lips swollen and still shining from the other's mouth. I watch as she unzips him at the table, takes him in her hand under the white drift of a heavy tablecloth. He is ordering, but under the cloth, the heavy scent of chlorine, drop of semen at its tip like a dark jewel. I want to take it with my tongue but now they are in a taxi, his fingers in her, a doorway on a strange city street where he enters her against the cold brick, the images are too fast, the film snaps with the black curling edges of burning celluloid. She has slipped below the water and drowned me out.

It rises in me like a body surfacing from a lake's sandy bed littered with broken bottles and bones of dead fish. Those pictures are things only I know, that he and I shared. She has no right to them, to thumb through them like a smutty novel whose pages stick together. The heavy black glass cube of her cream is on the sink. Mocks me, solid as her presence here in what was my life. Obsidian dark, hiding the perishable. It topples, shatters on the tile. She sits up in her bath, hair hanging around her face like ropes of seaweed, ugly, eyes staring at the place on the sink where the cube was. The black shards of glass glitter in the fleshy ooze of the cream that snakes its way across the tiles. She cuts her foot as she steps out of the tub. Now her blood threads among the remains.

I watch her crouch naked, fumble under the sink for bandages. Her breasts hang slack, touch the mound of her stomach, and I am slender as a knife. Beneath the counter, her hands close around the box hidden behind the water pipes. It is not the bandages. She palpates the contours with her blind fingertips, runs them across the top. I can feel how strongly she wants to pull it out, to bring into the light what she has found. I whisper through her wet hair, urge her, but she pulls her hand away. The bandages are right in front of her and, still kneeling, she puts one on her cut foot.

When she stands and confronts herself in the mirror above the sink, I stand behind her. She sees herself. I see nothing. Not even a shadow. But I gleam like a blade in the shards of glass on the floor.

We hear his car turn in the drive and I slip to the kitchen ahead of her. I want to go to him, but I have no voice, only a howl of wind that rattles the windowpanes. I dash them with my fury while she still trembles in the bathroom, naked and bleeding. With the opening of the front door, his smell floats through the rooms. He is solid, takes space that was empty a moment ago. I want to enter his eyes and see what he sees, curl in his mouth, be his breath. I circle him, trace his body with feathers torn from my wings. Arouse him, so he is ready for me.

He calls her name. She did not greet him as usual.

She is sitting on the couch wrapped in a silk robe. He looks at her swollen eyes, red face, and wonders. With a swift movement she grabs his hand, shakes it, demanding answers from him—the cold, the roses, the movements caught out of the corner of her eye, and now this afternoon, like something from a horror movie.

He doesn't say anything. He silences her with a kiss, smooth, he is unruffled water. He touches her breasts, between her legs, caresses to make her open. Finally she relents, rises from the couch, clings to him. Still kissing they stumble into the bedroom, her short laugh floats out of the dark doorway. The photographs on the mantle eye me. Looking at each of them, I try to remember who I am. There is only black reflection, an empty spill of water Narcissus cannot breach.

In the bedroom they are making love, her robe spread around her, red silken wings. He is on top of her, and I see her legs wrap around his thighs, her hands clutch him, force him to her rhythm. She arches her back. A shaft of moonlight illuminates her breasts. They are flesh. Limpid and white, falling over the contour of her ribcage, the nipples erect and wet from his mouth. She is not looking at him.

Instead she is intent on the corner I watch from. In the dark I see her teeth's moist gleam as she grins.

I enter him while he lies on top of her. I press her down. She can't breathe, is pulling at him, begging him to move. I press down harder, feel her breasts crush beneath me. With his teeth I bite her cheek. She cries out. I feel the gathering in his body. I pull out easily as he comes, listen to the words wrenched from him at his climax. He falls heavily onto her, but she pushes him off. It was not her name he called out.

She stumbles to the bathroom, and in the mirror sees herself taken by something she can't understand—the circlet of teeth marks on her cheek, branding her. She raises her hands to her head pulling back her hair, straining. Above her breast in the red of the silk, a small slit opens with her movement: a gash, clean-edged, as if cut by the sharpest of knives.

This morning she has left. These rooms are empty, except for him asleep in the spill of sheets. I watch. The sun, a sharp knife through the slats of the shade, cuts across his heart.

Neighbours

Astrid hated her new neighbourhood. When she had insisted on moving back to Toronto, she had envisioned small cafés, art galleries, little boutiques, all within walking distance. Sunday mornings she and Mark would be able to walk up the street and have croissants sitting in the window of a little bistro, reading the papers, people-watching. She would become fast friends with the two women who ran the little independent bookstore on the corner and spend happy afternoons browsing through the poetry section and reading her selections in an old dilapidated armchair while the dry-leaf smell of used books cosseted her and lulled her into drowsy contemplation.

All this was vivid in her mind as they looked through the houses for sale on the Internet, and then drove through the city with the real estate agent. Prices were high, houses were few, snatched up as soon as they went on the market, and Mark fell in love with this house just off of Eglinton West, a wide, unlovely major road, in a section of the city with strip mall storefronts that held wholesale clothing stores, dollar stores, nail salons and a No Frills grocery. There was public housing nearby, and cheap apartments in terrible high rises.

Astrid wished she'd never capitulated to Mark's whim, that she had held on to her vision of the city, but it was too late now. This was their neighbourhood.

Today Astrid was doing what she hated most, running errands on Eglinton. She rarely went out, unless it was to get on the subway and travel farther into the centre of the city to meet friends in their neighbourhoods near the university, or off the more affluent streets. Where she lived was a running joke with them.

God, why do you live out there? There's nothing there, unless you want fake nails or a Haile Selassie t-shirt. Where do you go out to eat? Jamaican Patty House?

Astrid always laughed along with them and said, oh the neighbourhood was changing, give it a few years and she would be the one laughing when her house appreciated and they were kicked out of their apartments because of rent increases. In reality, she despaired when she went out of her door. The neighbourhood *was* changing: more Latinos were moving in and the few remaining Portuguese and Italians were dying off or moving out. The bus ride to t he subway was a cacophony of Spanish and patois, reggae and rap. Her next-door neighbours rented out their basement apartment to a young man of indeterminate ethnicity, who Astrid was sure was a drug dealer. Other young men in hooded sweatshirts in low-riding cars came and went all times of the day and night and the tenant's girlfriend, who looked suspiciously underage, stood on the lawn and screamed and cried over several nights that summer. She also kicked in all the glass in his windows in her incoherent rage. Mark had confronted them when he and Astrid were woken up at four in the morning by their shouting, but that just scared Astrid. Who knew what those people would do, what they would break, next time?

She walked quickly up Eglinton, toward the Shoppers Drug Mart where the post office was; she had the manuscript of her next book of poetry in her bag. She walked past the fruit and vegetable markets in the ugly shops under the high-rise apartments. The overripe, spoiled scent of the goods crowded her the way the stores did themselves, with their wares in boxes and bins set out to the sidewalk's edge. The plastic hands in Lee's Crazy Nails waved at her, showing their elaborate three-inch nails with Canadian flags airbrushed on them and rhinestones placed in the centres of daisies. The wholesale clothing store (Open to the Public) on the corner displayed a hot pink t-shirt with *Baby Mama* written in gold script and a ridiculously short jean skirt with sparkling dollar signs on it. It was all so ugly. Astrid felt like she was going to cry; she wanted to go home, but she had to deliver this manuscript to her publisher. When she got home she would have a glass of wine and read, maybe some Proust or Flaubert.

In line at the post office section of the drugstore, Astrid began to feel a little better. She took out her manuscript and read a few pages while standing in line.

> *The city presses me to earth like a rough lover*
> *Insistent on its own rhythm*

I am a good writer, Astrid thought, and tucked the pages back into her bag. *There's that at least. Maybe if I make enough money we can move out of here. To a brownstone downtown, or a condo.*

Ahead of her was a woman with high cheekbones, the hair scraped back off her face in a low ponytail, its coarse ends neatly caught in a plastic clip. Her skin was the colour of—Astrid stopped. She couldn't describe the colour, even to herself, without getting into clichés, racial stereotypes. Coffee, chocolate, night—they'd all been used and generally by the wrong people. The woman's daughter was about three and swinging on her mother's hand. She watched Astrid, and Astrid smiled and gave her a little wave, but the child's measuring expression did not change, and abruptly she clung to her mother as if afraid. Her mother bent to her and whispered, and the little girl stood up and faced the counter where her mother had put a package that she was mailing. Astrid watched the child's small back, wing-like shoulder blades moving under her t-shirt, and saw the echo of the mother's strangely fragile back.

Then they were gone. Astrid mailed her manuscript, shopped for some lipstick and magazines and left.

At home, she poured the wine she had promised herself and sat down to read, but the wine made her sleepy and she nodded off, Proust slipping from her lap like a young child tired of being held.

Two days later Astrid sat in front of her laptop, frustrated, stuck on a line in her new poem:

What do pigeons know?

What *do* pigeons know? Who the hell cared what pigeons knew or didn't? Why was that line running through her head like some schizophrenic bus rider off his meds? She gave up and checked her e-mail. Someone had forwarded her a notice about a reading of some performance poet described as "Canada's own Anne Sexton." Astrid thought that particular poet was terrible. Always wearing a low-cut blue dress, the poet would get up on stage and make sexual sounds with her lips against a background of an electronic drum machine played by a man wearing no shirt. Everyone loved it. The poet got grants, was asked to read everywhere. Her book, called *Limerance*—mostly phonetic renderings of the sounds she made on stage arranged prettily on a page—sold out within two weeks of its first printing. Astrid felt privately that the author photo of the poet in her famous blue dress, barefooted, gazing out from under tousled hair with wide eyes, had something to do with sales. But Jesus, couldn't anyone see that the poetry itself was a crock with nothing behind it—just a gimmick, a clever persona?

Angry, she got up and went to the fridge. There was nothing there. She and Mark hadn't been to the grocery store in a week. She'd have to go up the street and get something, maybe some fruit, things for a salad; she and Mark definitely did not eat enough fruits and vegetables. Without making a conscious choice, she went into the first of the fruit and vegetable markets near their house. Most of the packaged foods she didn't recognize. Some had labels in Spanish or Korean, or strange names like Mr. Gouda, but she was only here to pick up produce anyway. Even so, there were still bins of things she had never seen before, or would have no idea of how to cook. She wandered down one aisle, noting how dirty the floor was, the dust on top of some of the boxes.

Just ahead of her she saw the woman from the post office again, looking at some cans. Her daughter stood beside her, clutching a box of cookies in one hand. The little girl looked at Astrid and then turned away to inspect the cookies. The woman stood very still and looked down at the can she was holding, her lips moving just perceptibly as she read the label. Again, her hair was pulled back, and Astrid saw the knifing arch of her cheekbones. The woman placed the can in her green plastic basket and, taking her daughter by the hand, walked around the corner of the aisle.

Astrid headed for the checkout, thinking, *the woman has never seen my face, but I have seen hers. She doesn't know I exist, but I know she does, and her daughter sees me, but doesn't care. It's like being invisible; I can see them and what they do, but they can't see me.* The thought excited her. She went home and returned to the line:

What do pigeons know?

And this time she had an answer and worked until Mark got home.

The next time she saw the woman was at the bus stop. She was not talking on her cell or with a friend, like so many other people did at the stop. She didn't have her little girl with her either. Astrid slid into the seat behind her and watched as the woman pulled a book out from a No Frills bag and read. Astrid couldn't see the title, though she craned her head, pretending she was reading advertisements. She did see the smooth nape of the woman's neck bent to the book, like the stem of a flower whose bloom was too heavy to hold up.

She wondered what the woman would do if she reached out and ran a finger down her neck. *Just tucking in your tag*, Astrid imagined herself saying; she would see the woman's face full on, and the woman would see her, maybe she would smile and say thank you, or maybe she would look at her as if she was crazy. Maybe she'd scream, and all the other passengers on the bus—talking loudly in foreign languages or listening to overflowing music on iPods, or just staring out the window—would turn and stare at her too, and then . . . they were at the Eglinton West subway, and the woman went down the stairway going north and Astrid went south, her mind ticking over the lines:

We split at the subway and I
Wonder where she rides
When I can't see her

Bad, they needed work, but Astrid felt a whole poem, maybe a new book, and held that with her for the rest of her ride.

For the next month Astrid saw the woman in the neighbourhood at various places, sometimes with her daughter, sometimes without. It didn't take her out into the neighbourhood more, searching for the woman; in some way, Astrid felt that would be cheating. Any glimpse of the woman had to be spontaneous, unexpected. The woman and her daughter were at the library, reading together in the late afternoon sun; Astrid watched from behind the stacks of New Arrivals. She saw them again at Shopper's buying toilet paper, then coming out of a little storefront church on another afternoon. One day she saw the woman alone, walking about ten feet ahead of her, coming back from the bus stop, and she watched her go up the narrow stairwell to the apartments above a nail salon. This gave Astrid a thrill. She knew where the woman lived and the woman had still never seen her. She stood and looked up at the apartment's windows and wondered what it was like. There was a curtain that looked like a flowered sheet in the front window; it moved slightly in the breeze from the street, the screen open to catch the first warm days of spring.

That night, Astrid dreamt of being in a florist's shop. The woman behind the counter was Asian and spoke no English. Astrid wanted to buy daisies to give to her woman, but all the Asian woman had in the shop were spiky, exotic plants that were much too tall or bulky for Astrid to carry.

Daisies, she shouted, in the time-honoured way of breaching language gaps, *daisies*, but the Asian woman just shook her head and pointed at a Bird of Paradise.

The next day Astrid wrote:

These blooms are too much for me
I need something I can hold in my hand
Something I can carry up narrow stairs
Where a flowered curtain . . .

Astrid stopped. Maybe, maybe not. She would have to put it aside for a day or two. She and Mark were going for dinner in the Annex, and she went to get dressed.

The next week was beautiful. On Thursday Astrid needed to go to the post office again, as she was mailing a grant application for a performance poetry piece she and her friend had conceived. They were planning on wearing black low-cut dresses and high-heeled sandals and reading their poems about failed relationships, while a saxophonist played in the background. Astrid had wondered if the saxophonist should be in a tank top, but she and her friend decided to have him in a tuxedo instead. There was already some interest in their piece for a festival out west. Astrid smiled at the Asian woman sweeping the sidewalk in front of the fruit stand; she nodded to the crossing guard at the corner who wore a turban and was comically serious about guiding her across the street if she was on his watch.

She knew she would see her woman today, and she was right. She was ahead of Astrid in line again. Today her hair was not in a clip, it straggled down her neck. She was mailing a letter, no, two letters. Her little girl was slowly circling her knees as they stood at the counter. When the girl came around the first time, Astrid smiled at her. She showed no sign of recognition. But when she made the turn the second time, she gave Astrid a little wave. Astrid waved back and felt that here was luck; she understood that things were going to turn, that she, Astrid, would have what she wanted—to be a good, respected writer, who was sought after and supported. The woman did not turn around, and she and her daughter left without Astrid glimpsing her face.

Next time, next time—oh, those poems are going to make me.

At home she wrote:

The shoulder blades like angel wings
Crossing and re-crossing as you stand
Oblivious to me but still
Offering you.

Astrid was pleased with the double play of still, the image of wings. She allowed herself a nap, in approbation of her own work.

When Mark got home, they had dinner. She told him about the poems and the grant, and they laughed and toasted her burgeoning career as a writer.

"Maybe you'll get that condo after all." Mark said, caressing her wrist. "I'm so proud of you."

While she washed the dishes, Mark turned on the news and she heard the faint murmur of the newscaster's voice. The dishes slipped beneath her fingers as she thought of new lines for her poems and she piled them on the draining board while whispering the lines to herself.

She heard the newscaster say, ". . . and today, in a tragic turn of events, a woman and her child jumped from an overpass into rush-hour traffic."

One glass bounced from her hand against a plate and cracked. Drying her hands on a towel, Astrid threw the glass in the trash and walked into the living room.

Their pictures were on the screen. A studio portrait of a mother and child. Those cheekbones making the standard mottled blue backdrop exotic and strange, the child looking up at her mother's face.

For the first time, she saw the woman's eyes.

"Turn it up, Mark."

But he misheard, and turned it off.

Their faces dwindled to a bright dot, then to nothing on the impenetrable black screen as Astrid stood and stared.

The Beautiful Boy

The boy came to her across the green grass. He was carrying a bouquet of rather sad-looking flowers.

Probably picked from some unsuspecting neighbour's lawn, she thought. She was wearing her usual uniform. Knee-length corduroy skirt, t-shirt and cardigan and always the scarf, the scarf.

She held her head at an angle and watched the boy. He was young with dark curls, his limbs browned from the summer, smooth still, his face not spotted with acne, his lips full and his cheeks pink. He moved with the ease of a boy who played sports, who ran and jumped and swam. She sat down on the small bench beneath the tree, the bench with a bronze plaque on it that some well-meaning person had put up in memoriam of something or other, and waited for him.

He handed her the flowers and she could smell his boy scent—the crushed green grass, chalk, sun, wind, dirt scent of him.

"For you, miss."

She took the flowers from him and patted the

bench beside her. "These are lovely. Sit down and tell me about your day."

He sat beside her and, kicking at a little hummock of dirt, told her about the reptile man that had come to school and shown them all a snake, a boa constrictor.

Huge like a fireman's hose, miss.

He told her about the baseball game during gym class, how he had hit the ball to the back fence. And he told her about looking out the window during math and seeing the tree they were under right now, with all the black birds gathered in its branches. The lady listened, her face soft; at one point she put her hand out and smoothed a curl away from Aaron's forehead, a gesture he never would have stood for from his mother. The light had dimmed a little and the air had cooled down; Aaron said it was time to go or he would be late for dinner. She watched him run across the field. He turned back once to wave and then went on. She didn't move from the bench.

At home, Aaron's mother asked him where he had been. Since his brother Nick had turned sixteen and begun dating girls, hanging out with them on the weekends, his mother had become suspicious of each son's movements. She hated the girls Nick brought to the house, especially the one called Susan.

That little whore, his mother had said. *Why don't we just get you a prostitute?*

Nick was embarrassed by his mother's constant insinuations and was out of the house more and more. Her face was haggard and drawn these days, her eyes glittering.

"I asked you where you were, Aaron." She was making dinner—Nick's favourite, macaroni and cheese. A piece of her hair straggled down over one eye, like a little dry snake. Aaron thought about the lady and her pretty soft hair that blew in the wind.

"Oh, hanging out in the field by the school."

"Well, next time try to make it home earlier or I'll send your brother after you."

Aaron's brother glared at him. After dinner, during which their mother had fussed at Nick, making sure that he ate enough, Nick cornered Aaron.

"Don't play in that field. I don't want to have to come in and get you. I've got things to do after school, and chasing after you isn't one of them. She's already all over my case all the time." His brother punched him on the shoulder and went up the stairs. Aaron trailed after him, running one hand along the banisters, rubbing his shoulder with the other.

"Hey Nick, how 'bout we play Xbox or something?"

Nick didn't answer. He slammed the door to

his room shut. Aaron stood outside it for a minute, until he heard Nick's CD player go on. He kicked his brother's door and went to his own room to get ready for bed. Later, he heard his mother knock on Nick's door. His brother roared for her to go away.

"You let me in right this minute, Nicholas Marks."

Aaron heard his brother's door open and his mother and Nick arguing. He couldn't make out the words. Since their father had left two years ago, their mother had watched them like hawks, Nick especially. As if she was afraid they would both disappear. She often accused them of being just like their father.

Aaron remembered when his father had still been at home. His mother had been sweet then. Happy, smiling and soft. She had laughed a lot and called Aaron her beautiful boy. Aaron had once seen his mother and father dancing in the living room, when they thought both boys were asleep. In the low light of a table lamp they had danced, holding each other tight, the music they were listening to giving them a quiet swaying rhythm. His father had kissed his mother and in the shadows they looked like one figure. Six months later, his father had left. He had met someone else, their mother had told them, someone online. She cried for weeks, became distant, and then her attention became almost unbearable, as she inserted herself into every part of the brothers' lives.

That night Aaron dreamt of the lady in the field. She was sitting in the highest branches of the tree. She wore a golden crown and shoes with diamonds or something on them; they sparkled as they swung above Aaron's head. She looked very pretty with her light brown hair blowing in the breeze, the gold crown catching the sun. Her cheeks were rosy and she was smiling.

Aaron was crossing the field toward her and he was bringing her something, something she wanted more than flowers. The grass was as high as his knees and he could hear the sharp saw of grasshoppers hidden there in the green. She smiled down at Aaron and he smiled up at her. Birds were singing nearby and he could hear them in the branches of the tree. The lady began to whistle and one of the birds landed on her wrist, a tiny sparrow with a bright, knowing look. It cocked its head as if listening to the lady, and then hopped to her shoulder and began to peck at her cheek.

Aaron watched in horror as the sparrow pecked on, the hole in the lady's cheek growing wider, its edges ragged. Blood began to ooze out, and then the sparrow plucked at her eye. The lady did not move.

She was still smiling, whistling a tuneless song that drew Aaron nearer, even as he tried to get away.

The next morning their mother was up early. She had made them waffles, something she hadn't done in a long time. She was smiling when Aaron came into the kitchen.

"Where's that sleepyhead brother of yours?" she asked, putting a plate down in front of Aaron.

"He was still in the bathroom when I came down."

"Trying to make himself gorgeous for all the girls at school, I bet." Though his mother tried to sound lighthearted, there was an undertone of something darker in her voice. Aaron glanced up at her. She was frowning at nothing, staring out the kitchen window.

"These are great, Mom." Aaron took another bite, grinning at her, hoping to break this mood before Nick came down.

"Well here he is, the high school Casanova," his mother said as Nick came in the doorway. She yanked out a chair for him and he sat down. Then she slammed down a plate with waffles. Abruptly, her mood seemed to lighten. "Did you sleep well, sweetheart?" She brushed Nick's hair back off his forehead. "God, Nicky, you are getting so handsome. You're starting to look so much like your father."

"For Chrissake, Mom, stop touching me." Nick jerked out from under her hand and stood up.

His mother pulled her hand away as if burnt. "Stop touching you? I like that. I'm your mother, young man, and you are the man of the house now. You better start acting like it." Her voice had risen to a shrill screech.

"Oh, just fuck off." Nick grabbed his bag and stormed out the door. Aaron got up.

"So you're leaving too, are you?" His mother sat down heavily at the table.

"Mom, I've got to go to school."

"*Mom, I've got to go to school.*" Her voice was mocking, and Aaron's heart turned cold. "Well, get out of here. And get right home tonight, do you hear me?"

Aaron hurried out the door, not looking back at his mother. He wished he knew where his father was; he'd call him and tell him to come home. But Nick wouldn't talk about it and his mother hadn't said anything.

At school, Aaron sat dreaming in his math class. He thought about his mother and wondered what she would be like tonight. He was afraid she would leave them too and then they would have to be put in foster care or something. Sometimes Aaron hated his father. It would come over him like a rain cloud, his heart tight; he'd want to hurt someone, but today he only felt sad. Why couldn't he be enough for his mother?

He looked out into the field through the classroom windows. It was a green expanse of grass, a little long, as if it wasn't mowed very often, nice and flat. The tree where the lady usually was, the one with the bench under it, was at the edge of the field, and beyond that were more trees. The lady's tree stood just a bit apart from the thicket, as if it had started to move toward the school a little, an advance scout for an army of trees that would sneak up on the brick building one night and surround it.

Aaron couldn't see the lady by the tree now, just the bench, and the birds in the branches coming and going. It reminded him of his dream and he thought he probably wouldn't go to the bench after school. He would go right home. At the front of the class the teacher droned on and Aaron watched the birds circling the tree and disappearing among the green of its leaves.

Aaron left school determined not to go see if the lady was under the tree. Nick would kill him if he was late again, especially if he had to come and look for him. He walked on the sidewalk across from the field and tried not to look out into the emerald expanse of it.

Out of the corner of his eye, he saw a movement. It was the lady. She was waving to him. Involuntarily, Aaron waved back. He stopped and looked fully at the field. Today the lady wasn't sitting on the bench; she was leaning against the tree. Something in her posture looked so sad that Aaron felt his heart tug. Why shouldn't he just go say hi? Was he that frightened of a stupid dream?

As he stood there, uncertain, he heard a tuneless sort of whistle. It made him think of cars, and summer, and pretty girls with long brown hair. It reminded him of the Christmas he got his XBox and the time Nick and his friends had let him hang out with them all afternoon and never once treated him like a kid. The whistle came from the field and he had to follow it.

The lady was waiting for him. She had her head cocked in that questioning way she had, like a robin in the grass listening for its dinner. Something about her today reminded Aaron of his mother back in the good days. Today the lady was wearing a green silk scarf around her neck, almost the same colour as the field.

"Hello, Aaron."

"Hey." Aaron sat down on the bench. For some reason he was a little embarrassed. He couldn't believe he had been frightened of coming out here. He ran his fingers over the plaque on the back of the bench. It read *In Memoriam: Elizabeth Ammon, teacher, 1965.* The letters felt cold under his fingertips. He pulled his hand back. The lady came and sat beside him.

"I wasn't sure you were going to come to see me today, Aaron."

"Oh well, you know." Aaron couldn't look the lady in the eye. "Hey, did you know this Elizabeth Ammon person?"

The lady took Aaron's hand. Aaron started—it was the first time the lady had ever touched him. Her fingers were smooth and cold. She didn't seem to notice his reaction.

"Let me tell you a story, Aaron."

She hadn't turned to him, was still staring across the field.

"Once there was a Queen who fell in love with a Prince. I know, already the words are wrong, the Queen should fall in love with a King, or with a Knight, or a Magician, anything but a Prince. Right, Aaron?" But she didn't wait for his answer before going on.

"He was a beautiful prince. Young, handsome, just about to be a man, voice breaking, some down on his face, but not yet a man with all their bad habits and arrogance. He was sixteen. Although the Queen had a King, she fell in love with the Prince, and they became lovers. You know what that means, don't you, Aaron?" She looked at him for the first time.

Aaron could feel himself blushing. He mumbled yes. His brother had sometimes shown him porn sites on the Internet. Aaron thought they were gross, but they had stirred a mixture of complicated feelings in him. The thought of the lady doing anything like that made him a bit sick; it was like thinking of his mother doing those things. He desperately wanted to pull his hand away, but she was gripping it tightly and he didn't want to hurt her feelings.

The lady searched his face. "I don't mean just that, Aaron. They exchanged letters and went for long walks. They felt that each had found a soulmate in the other, although their age difference was twenty years. The Queen and the Prince would meet day after day under this tree, and plan what they would do when the Prince left school and the Queen was free." The lady sighed and finally dropped Aaron's hand.

"But the King found out. He told the Prince's parents and the Queen was called before the court. She was sentenced to prison for corrupting a minor and lost her freedom for six long months. When she got out, no one would have her. She had lost everything."

Aaron was caught up in the story despite himself. "What happened to the Prince?"

For a moment the lady's face was terrible, her

mouth pulled down and her eyes narrowed with hate. "The Prince was sent to a kingdom far away and never called or wrote the poor Queen. He married a Princess in that kingdom and now has a home and children somewhere far away."

Aaron drew back a little. "But what does all that have to do with Elizabeth Ammon?"

The lady's face fell back into its usual delicate lines. "Aaron, I was trying to tell you. Elizabeth Ammon was the Queen. After the Prince abandoned her and there was nothing left for her anywhere, she hung herself from this tree."

"The Queen was a teacher?" Aaron was still trying to get his head around the story.

"Yes, Elizabeth taught at your school, the elementary."

There was a shout at the edge of the field.

"Oh shit." Aaron jumped up.

"Who's that?" the lady asked, shading her eyes to see to the sidewalk.

"That's my brother. He's supposed to get me if I'm late again."

"Your brother? How old is he?" the lady asked.

"His name's Nick. He's sixteen. Well, thanks for the cool story, but I've got to go now." Aaron picked up his book bag from beside the bench, and then he felt the lady's hand on his arm.

"Aaron, you'll be sure to come back and see me,

won't you? It gets a bit lonely sometimes. And bring your brother. I'd love to meet him."

Aaron ran across the field. He could see his brother standing on the sidewalk, waiting for him. Nick was glaring; even from far away Aaron could tell, but he didn't care. He felt as if he could do anything. As if the lady, by telling him the story, had given him her secrets and he had to protect her. Maybe somehow this would make everything right again. Maybe if their mother left them, they could live with the lady. Nick grabbed him by the collar when Aaron reached him.

"You stupid fuckface, I told you to stay the hell out of that field. If I get in trouble 'cause we're late, you're dead meat."

"Let go." Aaron shrugged out of Nick's grasp and swung his book bag at him.

"Who were you talking to out there?"

Aaron didn't answer Nick and started walking home.

"Look, Aaron." Nick grabbed his arm hard and swung him around. "That field is bad news. Some teacher hung herself there. She was fooling around with one of the guys from the high school and they sent her to jail or something. When she came out she killed herself 'cause they wouldn't let her teach and the guy's parents had sent him away. They say a bunch of different kids, all boys, have gone missing there. That's why no one uses it. Even the school knows it's fucked."

"I know." Aaron was gratified by the look of surprise on Nick's face. "What, do you think it's haunted or something, Nick?" He watched his brother closely. Nick's cheeks reddened. "I never guessed you were such a pussy, Nicky. I thought you were the man of the house now."

Nick let go of Aaron, and took a step away. "Just stay the hell out of that field." He walked ahead of Aaron, not looking back. Aaron followed, enjoying the sense of power their exchange had given him. He would never tell Nick about the lady, not now.

That night, Aaron had another dream. He was in a castle. The walls and floors seemed to be made of branches, leaves woven tightly together, branches with sharp little ends sticking out here and there. *For protection*, Aaron thought. Birds flitted through the corridors. Aaron began to mount the stairs to the main tower. They were made of polished wood and Aaron went up slowly. He heard the tuneless whistling of the birds as they flew past his head up into the upper reaches.

The lady was waiting for him in a chair with apples carved on the ends of the arms. She was looking out the window. When Aaron came in, she

turned to him and smiled. "Ah, Aaron, my page."
Aaron knelt before her. "Would you like to be my
champion, Aaron?"

Aaron nodded. The lady stood and picked up a
sword that lay next to the chair. It was green, with
rubies in the hilt that glistened like pigeon's eyes.
She touched him solemnly on each shoulder and the
top of the head with the sword and then said, "Arise."
Aaron stood. "Now, Aaron, before you become a full
knight, you must go on a quest. Bring me the thing I
want the most."

She untied the green scarf from around her
throat. In the bright sunlight Aaron could see the
terrible wound there. She handed the scarf to Aaron
and he tied it to his belt loop. The lady whistled,
the sound of someone blowing through two blades
of grass, the sound of long lazy days in the sun, of
those pure brief moments of happiness of being a
boy—and Aaron listened. He crept into the lady's lap
and laid his head alongside her cheek. Her breasts
in the flowing dress she was wearing were like the
apples carved on the chair. He tentatively reached
out a hand and touched one. She just smiled down on
him. Aaron became bolder. He cupped the soft swell
beneath the velvet of her gown.

Then he tried to kiss her on the lips, but she
turned her head and said, "Ah no, Aaron, you are too

young. You must be my knight, you must bring me my Prince." Aaron moved his hand off her breast and slid down from her lap. He was trembling.

He knew what he must do to please the lady.

Aaron stood beside the lady, underneath the tree. School had ended some hours ago, and still they waited. Aaron wore the lady's green scarf wound around his wrist. Nick came, and stood at the edge of the field. He called to Aaron, but Aaron did not move.

Instead he cupped his hands around his mouth and shouted back, "No, you come *here*. Are you a coward, Nicky? An ass-ugly coward? A mama's boy?"

Nick started to cross the field, but stopped. Aaron began to whistle and Nick came through the green grass, slowly, as if against his will. The lady put her hand on Aaron's shoulder and together they whistled Nick in. Aaron glanced at the lady's face— she was smiling and he knew he had done well. He was bringing her what she wanted most in the world. Afterward, Aaron would be the man of the house. His mother would knock on his door at night and they would dance in quiet circles while he kissed her lips. Slowly, Aaron untied the scarf from around his wrist and watched Nicky wade through the overgrown green to reach him.

Winter

The first notes fell after lunch while Sue cleared the table in the kitchen. They were written on rough newsprint, the kind they give kindergartners to colour on. The notes landed soundlessly among the dishes, crumpled napkins and crumbs, the way the last leaves of fall land on cold ground. She could make out something scrawled on them, but she didn't want to touch them. Instead she called Jim in from the other room.

"What the hell?"

He picked up a note and unfolded it. In pencil were unsteady loops and lines, like a child's first attempt at letters. He dropped the note back on the table and climbed on a chair to inspect the ceiling. A few last notes fluttered to the table and then they stopped. He unscrewed the light fixture, but it was a flush-mounted light that had come with the apartment. There were no open spaces or holes beneath it. He tapped the ceiling with his fist, but it was solid.

"The window, check the window."

Sue went over to the window, but it was firmly fastened. "It's locked, Jim."

Jim climbed down off the table. Sitting in a chair, he unfolded the notes one after another, placing them in a pile at his elbow as he glanced at each one.

"Sue." He looked up at her standing against the window, thin in a t-shirt and jeans, her face pale with fright. "Did you do this?"

The late winter sun coming feebly through the window washed the shadows out of her face, so that she looked bleached, like a faded photo.

"Of course not. I'm not a magician. How would I be able to make them come out of thin air?"

Jim nodded and continued to look through the notes. Sue sat in the chair opposite him.

"What do they say?"

"Nothing. Just these weird loops and scratches. Maybe they blew in through a heating duct some-where. There's kids in this building, right?"

"Four of them. The Sanjat twins on the third floor, they're about eight. Lori David is four, she's in apartment 5B, and the Porters just brought home their new baby, a boy, I think they're going to call him Sam. . . ."

Jim cut her off with a wave of his hand. "Could have been any of those kids. They all live above us. Someone was drawing too close to a heating vent, that's all."

He picked up the notes and walked over to the trash.

"Not the baby," Sue said quietly. "It couldn't have been the baby."

"Of course not."

The notes went in the trash and Jim left the kitchen. Sue just sat for a while at the table.

They had moved into their apartment five years ago, when they first started living together. A year later they married and now they were saving up for a house. The apartment was small, two bedrooms, but fine for a young couple with no children who were on their way up and out. They painted it and kept it clean, but the furniture was castoffs from their families, the plates and glasses mismatches from Goodwill, the towels thin and thready. When they had their house they would start fresh, all new furniture and dishes, they would be set. Jim was already doing well at his company, a small computer firm. Sue managed a retail-clothing store in the nearby mall. She didn't like the odd hours and the late nights, but they were saving for the future, couldn't have a gap in their income while she tried to switch jobs.

Today was Sue's day off. One good thing about retail was being able to stay home on some weekdays. She didn't have to fight weekend crowds at the grocery store, or worry if a repairman was coming. Jim of course had gone to work.

She sat on the couch having a cup of tea. The latest copy of *Vogue* lay face down on the couch beside her, but Sue was watching the steam curl from the ceramic mug she held in her hands. Far away, Sue could hear a baby crying, the Porters' new baby. It sounded hungry, she thought. She put down her cup and listened. The crying was loud, not as far away as she had first imagined. Could Lori Porter be on the landing with the baby? Maybe going out? But the sound seemed to be coming from inside the apartment, not outside.

She walked into the bedroom Jim had fixed up as an office. The heating vent was on the floor beside his computer table. She knelt beside it and put her ear to it. The crying wasn't coming from the vent. She walked into the master bedroom and moved the night table out of the way. As she put her ear to the vent, it seemed as if the crying was coming from directly behind her. Now it sounded like an older child who was angry that something had been taken away from it. As she moved back to the living room, the crying followed her, demanding, inconsolable.

"What? What do you want?" Sue stood in the middle of the living room and called again to whoever was crying, "What do you *want*?"

She moved to the phone to call 911; she'd tell them a child must be trapped somewhere in the apartment building, it must be echoing through the walls. As she picked up the phone to dial, she heard a noise in the kitchen. Carrying the cordless handset with her, she went to the kitchen door. A low-pitched babble was coming from behind the swinging door, like a child talking to itself. Her body temperature plummeted from fear. She stood in front of the door unable to move. The babbling continued, and then a giggle.

It's only a child, she thought, pushing open the kitchen door.

The babbling stopped, cut off like a disconnected phone. Sue stepped into the room, the phone clutched in her hand. Along the yellow wall of the eat-in kitchen were great scribbles of crayon, loops and circles, furious lines. Sue stood and stared at them.

A voice whispered in her ear: "It's very strange, isn't it?"

Sue turned around, the breath hitching shallowly from her chest, but no one was there. She ran out of the kitchen, and in the bathroom with the door locked, dialled Jim at work.

Jim came home, looked at the scribbles, heard about the crying, the voice and said, "Well, it got that right, this is very strange."

He gave Sue a whiskey and a sleeping pill and put her to bed. Sue knew he thought she had done it all, even the notes the other afternoon, but she was too tired to care. And while they were asleep that night, their bed was covered with notes, this time on white paper, like a fall of snow that blankets everything while the world sleeps.

Each note said in red pen "ring around the rosy." There were about two hundred in all, and Jim stayed home from work. He called the police who came and took samples of the two notes, the earlier ones that Jim had pulled out of the trash, and the ones that had fallen in the night. They took pictures of the crayon on the kitchen walls, too, but seemed most interested in the fact that Sue had heard voices, that she had been treated for depression in the past.

There had been an abortion four years ago. Jim had said they weren't ready for a baby, that there wasn't enough money, there was no room, and Sue had agreed, at least in theory. It would have been tough, and they probably weren't ready. Unexpectedly though, she had suffered from depression. Long days in bed crying, not wanting to handle the knives in the kitchen drawers out of fear of hurting herself. Times when it seemed like carrying a five-hundred-pound weight just to get in the shower, so it was easier to stay in her pyjamas. Jim tried everything to make her feel better. Breakfast in bed, movies, candlelight dinners. He did all the housework, stayed home as often as he could. Finally, their family doctor had prescribed an anti-depressant and she had begun to climb out of the pit.

She had been off the pills for a year, and things had been good. She still cried sometimes, but it was usually clean sadness brought about by a harsh news story or a tearjerker movie, sadness that ended with a good meal, or a sunny day, but her fear of a return of that absolute sense of hopelessness remained.

The police left, and she and Jim sat in the living room on the couch.

"Jim, we have to move, I can't take this."

Jim looked at her. "Honey, not yet. We have to give it another year. I don't want to keep renting; it's throwing money away. We need to start building some equity." He took her hand. "I don't want to end up like my father, working all his life with nothing to show for it but a little trailer down in Tallahassee. We're almost there."

"We could find another apartment, just as cheap."

"Not in this city. The rental market is crazy and this place is rent-controlled, you know that. Plus the costs of moving. Just one more year, sweetie."

Sue began to shake her head, but a crash from the kitchen made them both start. They looked at each other. Jim held her hand tightly. Another crash and he was on his feet, Sue grabbing his arm.

"No, Jim, don't go out there. Call the police."

"They were just here." He started for the kitchen.

Sue followed behind him, scared to stay alone on the couch. Jim stopped beside the door.

They could clearly hear a man's voice saying: "It's very strange, very strange, things are happening, things are happening." The voice kept repeating itself as if it was on a loop. Jim pushed open the door and a pile of plates flew out of the open cupboard and landed at his feet.

"It's very strange."

Sue screamed and the sound echoed around the small room. Jim just stood and stared at the shattered plates.

That night they sat up all night with the lights on, but the apartment was quiet.

"I won't be driven out of my home," Jim said at one point, but they didn't talk much at all.

Jim was home alone for the weekend. Sue had gone to work. One of the things she grumbled about was having to work weekends, missing out on time with him. He didn't tell her that sometimes he wanted to be alone. Since the abortion, she had been clingier than ever and it seemed he couldn't even get the time to just think, to relax.

Today he was painting the kitchen. The place had been quiet, and Jim had convinced himself that some freakish combination of old pipes, street noise and heating vent tricks had caused the phenomena. He took a long swallow of the Heineken sitting on the kitchen counter, stood back and surveyed his work. The crayon marks were gone and the new paint gleamed. Outside the kitchen windows snow fell softly and the bare trees made black scratches across the winter silver sky.

He knelt down to scrape the roller off into the paint tray when he heard a banging under the sink. The pipes.

He left the roller in the tray and opened the double doors under the sink. More knocks. Jim bent down to see what was going on under there. Something dark scuttled past his range of vision.

"Christ, a rat?"

He stood up and got the flashlight from the drawer next to the stove. He bent down again and shone it under the sink. Nothing there: no rats, no nests. Just some cleaning supplies, some rubber gloves.

"Losing your marbles, Jimmy boy. Your crazy wife is getting to you."

He stood up and shut the doors. He grabbed the Heineken and took a long swallow, turning back to his cleanup. The beer came back up in his throat.

There was something sitting on the kitchen table, something dark and formless. He walked over to it slowly, his heart counting every step he took. It was a doll, a child's gollywog. Black cloth with a grin, a red checked shirt, braids of cotton.

"It's very strange, isn't it?" The voice began to repeat over and over, until it was nothing more than babble.

Jim dropped the awful doll and backed out of the room. In the living room he sat on the couch. Listening to the voice still rambling on in the kitchen, he began to cry.

The living room was already filled with boxes. Sue worked on the office closet. Jim had already packed his computer papers and books, and she was boxing up the old sports gear and photos they kept in the closet. She pulled down a box from the top shelf and as it slid down, a newspaper floated to the ground. She put the box down and picked up the paper. It was yellowed, the date forty years earlier.

"Children Missing," the headline shouted in spiky black letters. Five children, ten children, the article gave names and ages; no one knew what had happened, no clues at this time. They hoped they would find at least one of them before they froze to death in the rapidly dropping temperatures.

Sue got up on the step-stool she had been using and searched the top shelf; nothing else, just that old paper. She got down and, still carrying the paper, went into the living room where Jim was boxing up the last of the CD collection.

"Jim?"

"Yes, honey?" He looked up from where he was kneeling.

"I'm pregnant."

In the kitchen stones began to fall, materializing from thin air and then hitting the Formica counter and worn linoleum with a sound like the cracking of tree branches under the weight of ice.

His Ghost

He knew they were soulmates the first time he saw her. She walked into class wearing something floaty. Brown? Black? It bothered him later that he couldn't remember the colour exactly, or the style of her clothing; he only remembered it was dark and seemed to float around her. He hoped that she would sit next to him, but she sat on the other side of the horseshoe of desks the teacher had arranged, and that turned out to be all right because then he could watch her face. It was small, surrounded by a quantity of blonde curly hair. She had very mobile expressions and he was sorry he couldn't freeze her face in its pretty perfection.

He wanted to tell her, *Don't wrinkle your nose like that, don't squint your eyes, don't open your mouth so far when you laugh, they ruin my picture of you.* But it was only the first day of class and he didn't even know her name.

Greg had been going to school in a desultory fashion for three years now. So far it had been a disappointment. His parents, not immigrants, not poor, had paid for Greg to have this chance to find himself.

"Take four years, my boy," his father had told him, clapping him on the shoulder at Greg's high school commencement. "Be on your own, get up to nonsense with some girls and some radical ideas."

The unspoken codicil to this was that after university, Greg would then of course "settle down." Maybe join his father in the architecture firm he owned, maybe not, but anyway find a real job.

Greg had vague ideas about writing. That's what he wanted to do. He pictured himself fairly constantly on a train, writing in a notebook, looking out of the window at passing scenery, then writing again. Sometimes a woman sat across from him. She often wore a hat, and was usually from a noble French family. They made love in the train's swaying compartment, with the shades pulled down, interrupted by the porter's knock, which would translate into his alarm shrilling away on his bedside table. So far, Greg had written nothing. Finally he had signed up for a twelve-week evening course in creative writing for third-year students. He hoped his muse would find him there. He usually pictured her as a large-breasted, rather old-fashioned woman, wearing a clingy gown of some silky material, similar to his mother in her wedding photos. He knew now that his muse was this blonde girl who had just walked in, wearing a brown top and a skirt of insubstantial fabric that swirled around her legs, so that she seemed to glide rather than walk.

That first night he learned that her name was Alison. In the coming weeks, although he would hopefully leave a seat empty for her on his right, by slinging his arm across the back until she came into view, she always sat with two other girls: Traci and Julie. The three of them spent their time together, writing notes back and forth to one another. He doubted that they listened to much of what the professor was saying, but they did bring in completed assignments. Alison was a competent writer, but he also thought that she spoiled some of her loveliest lyrics with her rather mordant sense of humour. When they were asked by the professor to comment on each other's work, Greg didn't spare her his ideas about her writing. If she would listen to him, she might actually be publishable in one or another of the literary magazines the teacher had recommended. But as far as he could tell, she was getting in her own way by not paying his thoughtful advice a bit of attention.

❧

One Wednesday night, to celebrate the halfway mark of the class, the whole group of them decided to go out for a drink afterwards, to continue the talking and critiquing that had gone on in the classroom. In their cozy circle in the half-light of a campus pub, there was the feeling that they really were writers, that among them might just be the next Dylan Thomas or Sylvia Plath, or if they were really good, even the next J.K. Rowling. Greg believed that he was the dark horse of the class, the one whose writing would have a depth and meaning that no one had seen at school, but that would be recognized by those trained to recognize such things: editors, publishers, *The New Yorker*.

He finagled himself a seat at the same table in the pub as Alison, squeezing in beside Julie and Traci. He noticed that Julie gave Alison a meaningful look. Alison rolled her eyes.

"So, Greg, what did you think of Alison's story tonight?" Julie asked him, taking a sip of her beer and looking at him with wide eyes. For a moment Greg thought Julie might have been his soulmate if he hadn't known that Alison was from the first minute he saw her. Julie was dark-haired and had blue eyes that were startling against her white skin. But she also had that strange mole on her chin and Greg knew his soulmate didn't have moles.

"Well," Greg said, settling back against the faux-leather banquette, "it was good, but then she had to put the description about the clown in there and it took away from the tension of the love scene between the ringmaster and the midget. Otherwise it might have had overtones of, say, John Barth."

"Really, you think Alison writes like John Barth?" Julie said. Beside her, Traci sniggered into her drink.

"At times, a very pale imitation, but there is something of his style in there." Greg took a sip of his own whiskey and water, none of that frat boy beer for him. He very much doubted that Julie, Traci or even Alison had ever read any John Barth.

"What do you think, Alison?" Julie said, turning vivaciously to her friend, whose determined stare was focused on a group of students at another table. "Do you think Greg has got it right?"

"I really don't want to talk about my writing." Alison gave Julie a small punch on the arm.

Julie rubbed it, narrowing her eyes, and said, "Sorry. I just thought that you might want to hear what Greg has to say. He's always so interested in your work."

"Yes, why is that, Greg?" Traci asked, looking up from her drink. "What is it about Alison's writing that fascinates you?"

Alison got up abruptly. "I'm going to the bathroom." She left the table, making that little grimace that Greg hated to see on her face; it marred the clear line of her nose, which could almost be called retroussé.

Traci repeated her question and Greg, wanting to reveal his secret knowledge of his compatibility with Alison, their inevitable deep understanding of one another, but at the same time wanting to keep it to himself for a while longer, thought about the question for a minute before answering.

"I think she's very talented. In some ways I think I understand her writing better than she does. She seems to have trouble with the real things of life, don't you think? Relationships, love, death. She always wants to make a joke of it. I really think she could be good if she would let go of the need to make everything meaningless."

Traci was taken aback by the sincerity of his reply. She looked at Julie.

"Wow, Greg, I guess you think about her writing a lot. What about mine?" Julie put her hand on Greg's arm.

"Too much sex," Greg said bluntly. "Can I get you two another drink?"

The next day, Julie friended Greg on Facebook. Greg accepted. He clicked on Julie's profile and went through her status. Single, looking for: whatever I can get, blah blah. Then he clicked on her photos. In her album titled "Crazy Lady Friends" he found pictures of Alison. There she was, with her arms around Julie, both of them mugging for the camera. Greg had never noticed the little freckles across Alison's nose; they really didn't suit her. She looked like Heidi or something equally kitschy.

There was a picture of her in a short black dress, wearing way too much eyeliner at a party. She was sitting on some guy's knee. Greg wondered who he was, but then saw that the date on the photo was last fall. Finally he found a picture of her alone, outside on campus. It was winter and she was wearing a pink muffler and hat. It must have been late in the day because the light was diffused. Her hair was in ringlets around her face and her grey eyes were looking straight at the camera. She had only a half-smile on her face and her skin was clear and ivory-coloured, except for the pink from cold across her nose and on her cheeks. She looked perfect, frozen in time. Greg clicked on the picture and added it to his own photos. That one was definitely a keeper.

"Is this seat taken?" Julie slid into the chair next to Greg. When Alison and Traci walked into the class, Julie waved to them. "Come on guys, we're gonna keep Greg company." Traci came over and flopped down on the other side of Julie, dropping her book bag on the floor beside her chair.

Alison looked around and started to head for a seat next to the teacher, but Julie said, "Alison, don't play teacher's pet, come on, there's a seat on the other side of Greg." Alison looked at Julie for a minute and then took the seat next to the teacher.

"God, what is up her butt tonight?" Julie whispered to Greg and Traci. She took out her notebook and started doodling on its cover. Greg got out the latest assignment, a 1500-word story about something that obsessed them. His piece was about his obsession with the diaries of famous people.

At the break, Greg and Traci went outside with Julie while she had a cigarette. Alison stayed inside talking to some of the other class members: a guy named David that Greg thought did far too much sci-fi writing and shouldn't be allowed in a serious creative writing course, and a fat girl named Nora, who Greg couldn't stand.

"Really, famous people's diaries? That's your obsession?" Julie blew a smoke ring in the air, tilting back her head so that the security light in the doorway made her black bangs shine and her eyes wash out into nothing. Her own story had been about her obsession with motorcycles. Traci's had been about cats. She lowered her head and took another drag on her cigarette. "I would have thought you would have chosen something else." Her voice had the choked sound of someone holding in smoke; then she turned her head away so that she didn't blow it in Greg's face.

Greg wondered what she was talking about. She was a strange one.

"Anyway, if you're so into diaries, you should totally check out Alison's blog. I'll give you my password because she only lets people she knows really well on. It's really good."

Greg was about to say something about Alison knowing him really well, but then thought it was probably true that she didn't yet know how close they were. He was sure she would let him on her blog eventually, but for now he might as well use Julie's password. Alison might still be shy, modest about the connection they shared.

Julie balanced her notebook on bent knee, the cigarette stuck in one corner of her mouth. Greg thought she looked like Popeye a bit, squinting over the smoke as she wrote. Popeye crossed with Olive Oyl. She straightened up and with a swift movement threw her cigarette into the gutter. Then she tore the page out and handed it to Greg.

"Here ya go, big guy, happy birthday. Come on kiddies, it's time to get back to class."

That night he read Alison's blog for the first time. She was no Samuel Pepys, Greg thought ruefully, but her writing did have a certain energy that he felt had potential. First Greg scanned the blog for his own name. He was a little disappointed when he didn't find it and then he scanned the blog for the name of any other man. He didn't find one. He then realized that even though her blog was supposed to be a diary, it had very little about people in her life, or even her own life.

She would say, for instance, that she really loved a certain type of chocolate and then would go off on a tangent about where that particular chocolate came from and what memories it brought back. Or where she had first eaten it, and then circle around to the best places to eat the chocolate—under a bridge, on a library bench—but even these types of memories were strangely unpopulated, with the rarely appearing people in them going under the generic names of, say, "a friend," or "this guy." It gave all of the people in her musings an insubstantial quality, as if to Alison, everyone was unreal except herself.

The longer he read, the more excited Greg became. He realized that even more than he had hoped, he and Alison shared the same disconnect from the people in their lives, the same understanding that very few people were "real" people. She was real for him and he knew that he was real for her. As he lay on his bed that night, he touched himself until he had his release for the first time in months.

Greg dressed very carefully before the next class. He wore his Ralph Lauren pink oxford shirt with Gap khakis and loafers without socks. Looking in the mirror, he thought he looked something like John Updike; then he grimaced, thinking that not one of the people in his class, in the whole of the Creative Writing Department probably knew who John Updike was. Well, he amended, maybe a professor or two, but certainly not the students who were all full of Stephen King and Stephenie Meyer.

Maybe, he thought, *I should dress like a vampire if I want to catch Alison's attention.* However, black velvet wasn't his style and as his muse she would not want him to be other than he truly was.

Alison wasn't in class. He slid in next to Julie.

"No Alison tonight?" He gave Traci on the other side of Julie a little wave.

"She's apparently freaked out because some nutbar has been leaving strange messages on her blog." Julie looked at Greg, her flat blue eyes on his. "That wouldn't be you, Mr. Greg, would it?"

"Hardly. Her blog was a bore, nothing of interest there."

"So I guess her diary won't be one of your obsessions then."

Greg looked at Julie; he wasn't sure what she meant. He gave a short bark of laughter. "Julie, Alison isn't famous."

"You can say that again." Julie opened her folder and took out her assignment. They had been asked to cut up a famous poem and put the lines back together, with a line of their own about everyday stuff between each one. She had chosen Baudelaire.

At the break they stood outside again while Julie smoked. Traci had a text message from Alison on her RAZR phone.

"God," Traci said, peering at the little screen. "She's really freaked out. She said she might call the police." She looked up from the phone. "Do you think it could be Chris?"

"Who's Chris?" Greg asked, inspecting his fingernails very closely.

Julie ground out her cigarette under the heel of one motorcycle boot, its silver chain glinting in the light. "Oh, this freak I used to date. After I dumped him he decided Alison was his type. She broke up with him about a month ago and apparently since then he's been writing her this love poetry and crap. I never figured him for much of writer. All we did was fuck." She laughed. "Sorry, Mr. Khaki Greg, didn't mean to shock you."

"Well, it's definitely not love poetry she's getting," Traci said in the timeless voice of a back-fence gossip. "Some of the stuff was really freaky, about dying together, and being soulmates and then saying she was an evil cunt and had to die."

"I'll call her when I get home tonight," Julie said, opening the doors to the building. "I know people who can trace that kind of shit."

Later that night Greg tried to go to Alison's blog, but it had been shut down. He sat at the computer, staring into the grey light of the screen. Someone else was writing her love poetry, his muse. He knew that in the night Alison was probably staring at the screen on her computer too; it was what they all did, e-mailed friends, surfed the Net, checked Facebook, watched YouTube, wrote on their blogs and spat out tedious one-liners on Twitter. Separate but close, able to feel only one's own realness since everyone else was just a name on a screen that could be turned on or off. Like a spider that sat at the centre of its web, he felt that if he could just twitch the strand that connected to her, he could reach her. She and he would stand out from all the others dancing at the ends of other strands, spinning out their connections endlessly.

He opened the folder from class. On the first day the teacher had given everyone a list of their classmates' e-mails. He would just send her a short note; offer his help, his support. His pale fingers moved across the keyboard as he typed in her address.

At the next class, Alison was there. Greg had worn a black turtleneck and jeans, thinking that it was closer to what someone in a Stephenie Meyer novel might wear without being too overtly Byronic. Of course, he had never heard Alison say she particularly liked vampires, or Stephenie Meyer for that matter, but all girls her age did, he'd seen the fan pages on Facebook. Julie raised one eyebrow when she saw him, the one she had recently had pierced. There was still a little red rim around the entry point of the tiny silver ring. Greg gave a little inward shudder. Mutilation, that's all it was. How anyone could think it was sexy or in any way appealing was beyond him.

"Looking good, Greg. Those khakis made you look like a middle-aged accountant." Julie whispered in his ear. He felt the fringe of her bangs brush his cheek. Her breath smelled of smoke.

Despite the turtleneck, Alison had sat across the room, next to Nora and David. Greg checked his iPhone quickly to see if she had maybe sent an e-mail in response to his latest one. There was no message from her. Even though the iPhone was in his lap, Julie snatched it from him. He felt her quick fingers there for a moment and then she was squealing.

"Oh my God, Greg, what is this? You totally stole the picture I took of Alison."

Everyone in the room turned.

"Greg, you have a total crush on Alison." To Greg, Julie's voice sounded ridiculously high-pitched. She held the phone out to Traci.

Traci, who had been staring at Greg since Julie's announcement and running a Chupa Chup around the inside of her mouth, pulled it out with a sucking sound and said, "He is totally blushing. Greg, that is so sweet. Alison you have got to see this. It's that one of you in the pink hat."

Greg cursed himself for making that picture his screen saver. Across the room, Alison had also blushed. Greg noticed that she blushed rather unattractively, with great uneven red patches across her cheeks. Alison made an attempt to laugh. "God, I always hated that hat. I never wear pink and it made me itch."

Greg, who had no idea where he got the courage, said, "I thought you looked beautiful."

Several of the girls in the class ahhed at that, but before things could go any further, the teacher came in and they all settled down to the business of•

learning how to be rich and successful writers.

At the break, Greg rather hoped he could have a chat with Alison, put her at ease. He had felt the connection in the class, and he knew she had too. Finally they could start to talk, to get over this false constraint that lay between them, like a . . . here Greg fumbled for a simile. "Ocean" was too obvious. Like . . . a broken grand piano. Alison had taken off, though, and Julie and Traci had suddenly shown an interest in getting to know David the Sci-Fi Geek.

Greg thought bitterly that maybe Julie was hoping to get David to put some of her pretentious Goth poetry in the horror magazine he supposedly edited. Or she was just looking to get laid.

Greg tried to send Alison one more e-mail that night. He wanted to apologize for the discomfort that the public revelation of their relationship had caused her, and invite her for coffee. Greg felt that in some ways the timing had been very poor, but in other ways he was relieved that they could now get past the awkward stage of pretending not to recognize one another and move right into talking about their future.

He fell into a reverie of their married life, of travelling together, renting a house in Florence where he would write and she would help him, editing his work, sending it out to magazines and grant committees. He would introduce her to the great writers, not to mention the opera, fine wines, the beauty of living at a certain aesthetic level. He had undone his fly as he daydreamed, and now as he pushed "send" on the keyboard with his left hand, he came into his right, pearls dripping from his fingers like the single strand he imagined gleaming around her neck when she walked toward him down the aisle.

The next morning, Greg's stomach dropped when he saw that he had received an e-mail. She had answered him.

But when he opened it, it said that his message had been undeliverable—the account did not exist.

At the last class they all had to read a piece of their work out loud, standing up in front of everyone. Their professor had insisted that a good deal of being a writer was being able to read your work in public. Julie and Traci flanked Greg as always, Julie's little serpent tongue occasionally flicking his ear as she whispered snide remarks about all their classmates during their readings.

"She's lucky she's fat," whispered Julie. They had been listening to Nora's memoir about being teased as a kid because of her weight. "She's so boring, she wouldn't have anything to write about if it wasn't for that."

When David read his piece about life on another planet, Julie said, "Oh, he is so wishing someone would probe his ass." Greg had a hard time not laughing at Julie's perceptive cruelty; she was simply saying what Greg privately thought. Traci on the other side giggled immoderately at everything Julie said, at least the bits she caught.

Alison had not looked at Greg for the entire class. When she got up to read, Julie whispered, "I bet she made all that up about a stalker just to get your attention." Greg looked at Alison who was wearing the same outfit she had worn on the first day of class. He wondered if maybe she was not the soulmate he had envisioned—she did seem a bit desperate for attention.

She read something about a woman who disappeared bit by bit. Greg almost immediately tuned her out; more sci-fi nonsense. He guessed he hadn't been far off with the Stephenie Meyer thing.

Julie leaned behind his back and he heard her whisper to Traci, "I wish *she'd* disappear, such a drama queen." Traci giggled again. Julie read some of her dark poetry. Really, Greg thought, if you could get past the rather messy, painful-sounding sex, it wasn't all bad. Traci read about her mother's addiction to prescription painkillers. Everyone applauded when she announced it had been accepted by a feminist review.

Julie whispered to Greg, "I gave her that idea; her mother's never taken a prescription painkiller in her life. She couldn't think of anything to write about."

After the class, they were all invited over to their professor's for drinks. He lived in a brownstone not far from the university. The students tumbled into cabs, laughing and talking about their nerves when they got up to read, congratulating one another on their work. Speculating about who would stick with writing, who would give it up to get a real job in IT or advertising.

Greg had brought a good bottle of single malt, having no hope for whatever drinks would be served at the party. He doubted that even a professor would be able to tell a so-so bottle from the really good stuff. He, Julie and Traci shared surreptitious swigs from it in the back of their taxi. Greg hadn't noticed what cab Alison had gotten into and found, surprisingly, that he didn't care.

The professor's ground floor was packed with students and other literary types he had invited along. Julie and Traci left Greg with his bottle of Scotch and went to pour themselves liberal drinks from the professor's supply of cheap red wine. Greg had to be satisfied with a plastic cup for his whiskey, though it really deserved cut crystal, but perhaps this was what the term Bohemian referred to. Julie and Traci came back to where Greg was standing, squinting at a pretty bad copy of a Tom Thompson painting hanging on the wall above a leather armchair.

"Chris is here," Traci said in a stage whisper.

"Who?" Greg asked.

"Julie's ex, the one that Alison dumped." Julie was standing next to Traci, staring at another corner of the room, her mouth thinned into a narrow line. The way she pulled her eyebrows together made the ring there stand out aggressively. Greg looked where Traci was pointing. He saw Alison having an animated conversation with a tall dark-haired guy in a leather jacket. He was shaking his head vehemently at whatever Alison was saying.

"I need a fucking smoke," Julie said. She downed the contents of her plastic cup in one swallow and threw it on the leather chair; the dregs of the wine splashed the wall behind it like tiny droplets of blood. Without looking at Traci or Greg, she went out the front door. Chris had walked away from Alison and she was standing there alone. Greg wondered if he should go and talk to her, if this would be a good time. But Traci beat him to it, scurrying over to Alison. Greg walked to the table that the professor had set up as a makeshift bar, near the corner where Alison and Traci stood.

He heard Traci say, "Greg is so sweet, you should just talk to him. He totally wouldn't do that."

A jostle of drunken creative types trying to get to the bar blocked out the rest of the conversation. Greg moved away from the crowd. He saw that Traci was still talking to Alison and Julie was nowhere to be seen. He went to the professor's bathroom, which was decorated with the covers of famous Can-Lit novels in gilt frames against mouse-brown walls. Greg found it a bit precious; he would have gone with off-white walls. While he was on the toilet, he took out his iPhone, just in case. No messages.

He came out of the bathroom and Traci was standing there. "She got another message! Greg, she is, like, totally freaked. He said some really nasty things this time."

Greg saw Alison struggling through the crush to the front door.

Traci said, "Greg, offer to walk her home or something. He could be anywhere."

Traci's words were like a sign. Greg knew that this is how he and Alison were supposed to finally come together. He would be her saviour. He rushed after her, elbowing people out of the way. He passed Julie standing out on the side of the front steps, smoking a cigarette, playing with her cell phone and talking to some guy with multiple piercings. She saw Greg hurry past and turned to follow his progress down the walk. Greg caught up with Alison on the front sidewalk.

He touched her arm. She gave a little squeak. "Alison, I'll see you home. You really shouldn't walk home alone."

Julie and Traci had come down to the end of the professor's path and were watching, listening to the exchange.

"Oh no, that's okay, Greg. I'm fine, I'm . . . that's my bus stop just over there, across the street. I'm . . ." She started walking away again, looking over her shoulder at him.

Greg saw the message there; she needed him to follow, to keep her safe. In three steps he was beside her. He took her arm. "Alison, at least let me walk you to the stop and wait with you." She pulled her arm from his and began to run, darting across the street.

The car hit her full on and Greg watched as she flew into the air, her airy brown skirt belling around her. Then she disappeared under the car's wheels.

That's the colour it was, brown. I wonder why I couldn't remember that. Greg thought. *I've never liked brown.*

Next to him he heard Julie breathe, "Oh shit." And felt her cold thin fingers snake between his.

That night he and Julie made love. Greg did not imagine Alison while he was on top of Julie; he only saw Julie's pale face with no freckles in the moonlight that came through his blinds. But he felt that Alison's spirit was near, approving of her two friends coming together to celebrate life after her death. Julie raised her chin as he moved above her and he saw that mole again. He wondered if she would consider having it removed.

It was six months after classes had ended that he first saw Alison.

Greg was on a train rocking through the South of France. He had convinced his father that a year in Europe after finishing college was what he needed, particularly after the trauma of losing one of his classmates, one he had been close to. He read the latest e-mail from Julie on his iBook. Traci had apparently decided to take women's studies and had started writing articles about her new lesbian relationship for an online women's zine. Her column was called "Lesbian and Loving It."

Julie was having her collection of poems published by a well-known publishing house. They were about losing a friend so young and the dark circumstances leading up to the event. The final section in the book was about the survivors and how they would carry on and overcome the loss. Rather like a modern-day

Tennyson's Arthur Hallam poems, Greg thought. Julie wrote that she had already been interviewed on several literary radio shows and there was a good chance she might be on some television show or other. She had had her mole removed.

Julie signed her e-mail "love," but Greg was already imagining the pale French girl he would meet. She would look like Marion Cotillard, but have the dimples of Audrey Tautou. He imagined her in a simple flowered dress, shopping in the market with a wicker basket. They would have rustic French meals, share bottles of good red wine and make love in lavender-scented sheets. Greg was looking forward to it. He logged off his iBook and closed the cover.

When he looked up, she was there.

At first he thought it was a trick of the sunlight filtering through the glass of the train's windows, but she became more solid as he watched.

Alison stared back at him. Her eyes were panicked and her mouth was moving. Greg felt she was trying to make a connection. He didn't feel any fear, but he couldn't make out what she was saying. He watched her eyes dart side to side and saw her close her mouth. It looked as if her lips were trembling. He noticed that her freckles had faded away, or were not visible any longer. She was wearing the pink hat and scarf he had so loved on her.

Wondering if this was just a momentary visitation

or if she would be with him forever, he opened his iBook and began to write, at first hesitantly, but every time he looked up and saw Alison still sitting across from him, her eyes on him as if she couldn't look away, he typed with more assurance. The story was about a woman that was so obsessed with a man that she followed his every move. She made up wild stories to get his attention and finally, in desperation, threw herself in front of a car so that he would rescue her. Of course, just as in life, it was too late, she miscalculated and the car killed her, rather than offering an opportunity for the man she loved to be her hero.

A week later Greg was sitting in a café in a small town outside of Nîmes, pointedly ignoring Alison. She had been following him like a lost dog hoping for a handout ever since the train had pulled into the station. He thought she would have faded by now. In public places she never sat with him, but rather hovered nearby as if waiting for him to invite her to take a seat. In private she usually placed herself as close to him as possible and tried to make herself heard. He couldn't stand the meaningless motions of her hands and mouth and he wondered how he could have ever thought she was his soulmate, his muse.

On the other hand, his writing had never been

going better, so he was a bit worried that if she left for good, the drive to write would leave with her. The thing to do, he knew, was to find his true muse, the live girl that would inspire him endlessly. As always, Alison's grey eyes were turned on him, pleadingly, desperate for attention.

Just like in life, Greg thought, *needy*. He turned his back on her and took a slow sip of his espresso. The sun and the heat, the quaint cobbled street and crooked buildings filled Greg with a sense of well-being. Alison had crept up to a table on his other side. Greg sighed. He wondered why in the hell she was wearing that pink hat and scarf; she hadn't had them on when she'd been killed. He was sick of them. They looked particularly ridiculous in this sun-drenched landscape.

A girl in a dress scattered with yellow flowers blocked Greg's view of Alison. She sat down at a table next to him. Her rich brown hair fell to her shoulders in waves and she had dark eyes. She glanced at Greg briefly and gave him a polite smile, then bowed her head over a book she took from her bag. When the waiter took her order, Greg noticed she answered in French, but with an accent. He drank more of his espresso, trying to relax. The girl raised her book up off the table and Greg saw that it was *The Witches of Eastwick*. Although it was his least favourite of

Updike's works, he felt the twitch of recognition. This was the sign: this was his muse, just as he had imagined.

Alison had drifted closer to the table where the girl was sitting. Greg looked up at her, annoyed. She seemed to be trying to catch the girl's attention— jealous, he knew—but thank God the girl didn't seem to notice her presence at all. When the waiter brought out the girl's omelette and her mineral water, Greg used the chance to surreptitiously snap a picture of her with his iPhone. She looked lovely on the screen, the sun on her hair, her face turned up to the waiter, smiling, almost perfect, Greg thought, except for the fact she had a slightly tip-tilted nose. Greg would have preferred a straighter bridge, a more refined tip. Perhaps she would consider seeing a plastic surgeon about it. As he was closing his phone, he noticed the photo of Alison he had taken off Julie's Facebook page.

God, what did I ever see in her? I thought I got rid of that thing. He didn't want to be to be one of those assholes, pretentiously playing with his phone; he would delete Alison later. He put the phone in his pocket and turned to the girl.

The dead Alison shivered and struggled between them, opening and closing her mouth like a fish. Greg knew she was probably mouthing "I love you" at him again. She tried to catch his eye, someone's, anyone's eye, making the same futile, clinging gestures she always did. Greg turned his chair toward his new muse, so he wouldn't have to see.

"Hello, I'm Greg." He held out his hand. His muse tentatively held out hers, then smiled as Greg took it.

Picnic

They found the shoe first. It was not a tennis shoe, like the ones you so often see on the side of the highway, sole facing the passing cars, laces trailing in the dirt. This shoe lying in the long grass under a tree was a silvery pump, with a little cluster of rhinestones on the toe. It reminded Abigail of a pair of shoes that she had coveted in an expensive store near their apartment, but that were out of reach of their budget. Mark picked it up.

"That's weird." He looked around in the tall grass for the mate. "How in the hell did it get here?"

"You won't find the other. Lost shoes are always single."

She took the shoe from Mark and turned it over in her hands to read the label. An expensive brand. "Too bad. It's even my size."

"Who wears shoes like these here?"

They had been on their way to their favourite picnic spot, off the highway, down a country road, then a turn-off and a short walk through some trees to an open grassy spot with a small creek running through it. Mark had never told Abigail how he knew about it. She suspected his last girlfriend, the one he called "the farmer's daughter," had brought him here.

"Someone very elegant, who probably brought champagne and Brie in a basket, not turkey and rye in plastic bags from the No Frills grocery store," Abigail said. "Should I keep it?"

"Hold on to it for a while, we may find the other along the way."

Abigail wasn't holding out much hope, but she found herself scanning the edges of the path as they walked. It was a nice shoe. But it was Mark who saw the clock.

"Holy shit. Look at this, just sitting here." Mark bent over and picked up a clock in a wooden case. What Abigail knew was called a mantle clock. Her grandmother had had one on the mantle in her house.

The clock Mark held was in good shape—the wood shiny with a fine grain; the face un-clouded, though the hands had stopped at four thirty. It was almost an antique. No one Abigail or Mark knew had a clock like it. It was something you inherited and they were not at that stage yet.

"I bet it would run if I wound it." Mark turned the clock around: "But it needs a key."

He handed Abigail the duffel bag with their picnic in it and squatted down. He sifted through the weeds and rocks where the clock had been waiting; no key. Abigail stood beside him toeing through the dirt in front of her. Finally, after about five minutes, Mark stood up. Abigail started off down the road and Mark had to hurry to catch up.

"Hold on Abigail, this thing is heavy. I want to put it in the bag."

Abigail stopped. "I think it's creepy."

"It's just a clock."

"But why is it out here in the middle of nowhere? I think you should leave it where it was."

"Come on Abigail, someone probably dumped it. You know how country people are, they don't care about this stuff."

He knelt down by the duffel bag, which Abigail had dropped on the path, and unzipped it. "I notice you're still carrying that shoe." He put the clock in the bag carefully, rearranging the sandwiches around it.

"Fine." Abigail tossed the shoe into the trees beside the path.

"I'm keeping the clock."

They walked on. Abigail didn't look at Mark. She wanted him to apologize, but he whistled and seemed unconcerned by the fact that she was maintaining the proverbial stony silence. She pointedly looked at the opposite side of the path, into the trees, which bent over them making an arch, like the ceiling of a cathedral. Some of the leaves were turning, looking like flicks of fire amid the green calm.

It was early September, which meant that she had met Mark almost exactly a year ago. They had been in a yoga class at the community centre in Abigail's neighbourhood. She had not expected any men to be there, as she imagined they thought of yoga as a sissy sport, preferring cycling or weight training. But there had been three men in the class. Two of the ponytail-Birkenstock type, and Mark. He was tall with brown hair that fell over one eye and a long, lean, muscled body. She surreptitiously watched him when he went through poses, especially enjoying downward dog, which was not as obscene as it sounded, but did accentuate his leg muscles and tight rear end.

There wasn't a ring on his finger, but Abigail knew that was no indicator of anything. Lots of men didn't wear their wedding rings. Two other women in the class had already engaged him in conversation and Abigail didn't even bother trying to compete, it wasn't in her nature.

One day while they were packing up their mats, Mark asked her if she wanted to grab a coffee with him at Starbucks. They went for coffee and then dinner, and two months later moved in together. Both of them were living with roommates who got on their nerves, and in the city they lived in, at their age, few people could afford to live alone. They figured why not live with someone you love at least. For Abigail it was wonderful, she had assumed Mark had felt the same way. Until today, they had never had a fight of any sort. She had never felt herself falling so easily into the stereotypical injured woman role, silent and unforgiving, or seen Mark being so . . . *male*, ignoring her, pigheaded. He took yoga, for God's sake.

Abigail turned to him to end the impasse and saw something hanging in a tree. She screamed.

Mark stopped.

Abigail started to laugh. "Oh God, that scared the shit out of me. I didn't know what it was." She pointed into the tree.

Mark looked to where Abigail was pointing. Suspended from the branch of one of the trees was a chair. A gold spindly chair, the type a lady would sit in at her dressing table.

Maybe, Abigail thought wildly, *wearing those shoes we found.*

Mark walked over to the tree, but tall as he was, he couldn't quite reach it.

"Give me a boost, Abigail."

Abigail went over and made a cup of her hands so that he could step up and grab the branch just below the one with the chair. He swung himself up, and climbed up another branch until he could reach it.

He unhooked the chair from the end of the branch.

"Bombs away," he yelled.

The chair hit the ground in front of Abigail. It was metal, with a blue tufted seat made out of vinyl. As a girl, her mother had had one in her bedroom. Abigail knew because it had been in their basement while she was growing up, until it was finally thrown out when the vinyl had cracked and the gold flaked off the back. Abigail didn't touch the chair. Mark clambered back down and picked it up with one hand.

"Want a chair?"

"It's not funny, it's scary. What the hell is going on?"

"I told you, people in the country just dump shit for no reason. Or they drag it outside to use at a beer party and leave it behind."

"Mark, this chair has not been sitting outside. Look at it." They looked at the chair, whose vinyl was so glossy you could almost see yourself in the surface. "That clock hasn't been outside for very long either. The shoe looked brand new. Besides, these things weren't here the last time we came." That had been in July, the height of summer. They had listened to cicadas and felt the heat on their bare backs when they made love on the picnic blanket.

Mark's mouth was set. "I tell you, they dump stuff."

"Who told you that, 'the farmer's daughter'?"

Mark picked up the chair and walked into the clearing. He put it down under a tree and sat down on it. His long male body looked ridiculous on the curvy chair with the short gilt legs. Abigail stood off to the side watching him. He unpacked the blanket and the sandwiches, set the beer bottles down beside the chair.

"Help me?" He indicated the blanket and Abigail went over to him, almost against her will, disgusted with his determination to be funny, to pretend this was normal. Someone's household or something was strewn all over, as if things had been dropped to lighten the load on a journey, or leave a trail for someone.

They snapped the blanket out between them and laid it on the grass. Mark took the beer down to the creek to sit in the cool water, and Abigail set out the sandwiches. He came back and dropped something in front of her. Three small silver teaspoons fell onto the dull red plaid of the blanket. Bright as if they had just been polished that day, a cursive D engraved on the handle. Drummond was Mark's last name.

"Found them in the grass."

Abigail picked one up, then let it fall back onto the blanket.

"Mark, did you do this? Tell me, I won't be angry."

For a minute she thought maybe he had, maybe this was some bizarre prelude to a proposal.

"Are you crazy?" Mark sat down in the blue and gold chair again. "When the hell would I have had the time to do this, and why the fuck would I?"

He was mad and Abigail knew it, but she couldn't stop herself. "Maybe the other night when you were supposedly out with the boys, maybe because you're trying to freak me out, maybe you're sick of me and are too cowardly to come out and say it. I don't understand why you're acting like this is so normal. I've been in the country before too and never seen spoons and clocks all over the place."

"Abigail," Mark said conversationally, "you're nuts. Even if someone did drop them here, they're just things, not harbingers of doom or some Hitchcock shit. I didn't put them here, and if you want to check, call Mike or Tim. They'll tell you I was at the bar with them. I wasn't even out long enough to have driven out here and back. And incidentally, I've gotten rid of girlfriends before without resorting to bizarre mind games. I tend to prefer the simple method of telling them I'm not in love with them anymore."

He looked at her and picked up one of the sandwiches off the blanket.

Abigail cried. She used the rough paper napkins to rub at the tears on her face. Mark just sat in that ridiculous chair, reading a paperback he had brought along and eating his sandwich. After a minute he got up and went over to the creek and got a beer, brought it back and sat down again. Abigail watched an ant struggle over the plastic wrap of the sandwich, trying to get to the meat inside.

She stood up and walked away from the picnic, toward a small birch tree.

The tree was beautiful. The white birch bark was peeling in some places to expose the pale pink of the underside, the oval leaves shivering, falling around her with each breath of wind. A framed photograph was propped in the crook of a branch. A man and woman getting married, but the glass was cracked, the photo faded and water-damaged. Their faces were barely distinguishable, though Abigail could almost make out Mark's fall of hair, and the silvery shoe that peeped out from under the woman's wedding dress. She put the photograph carefully back on the branch.

She turned from the tree and walked back to the picnic they'd spread out together in the middle of the forest. Mark had fallen asleep on the blanket, his chest rising and falling in long steady breaths. Abigail sat down on the gilt and blue chair. She reached down and took off her sandal. With one smooth motion she stretched out her leg and slid her foot into the silver shoe waiting there on the blanket next to Mark. It fit perfectly.

Twenty-First-Century Design

1

The house looked like so many concrete shoeboxes piled one on top of the other and dumped in the middle of some hapless farmer's field. There were bright blue metal pillars holding up one end and porthole windows along the front that watched them as their Escalade turned up the long drive.

"It's perfectly flat," Emily said, looking out the driver's-side window. "Not a tree in sight."

"The architect's vision, my dear, his house rising out of these flat farmlands. If you look closely, each of the sections of land is a different colour: brown, green, yellow. It's the decorative grasses he had planted."

"You sound like a brochure."

"I read it in *Architectural Digest*."

Emily giggled and they looked out the window at the flat land with the concrete boxes on it. From the back came the whispers of the television screens mounted onto the backs of the front seats, a standard feature with this model of Escalade her husband Ian had brought home a month ago. The girls were quiet, intent presumably on the Steve Martin version of *Cheaper by the Dozen*, one of those warm family-disaster movies so dear to the hearts of children.

"I wonder who keeps the grass so perfect?" Emily noted that each square of coloured grass was exactly the same height as the others. From above, she thought, the effect must be that of a particularly sombre patchwork quilt.

"A lawn service I'm sure." Ian loved the idea of living in an important building, he loved the fact that he was able to consider buying it. He loved being rich. Since his computer company had been bought out at an astronomical sum, and he had been kept on as head of development at a ridiculous salary, he had been dreaming of buying a showplace of a home. Not one of those new fifty-thousand-foot monstrosities, but something with pedigree, something with design cachet. This house was perfect. All the modern masters had influenced its architect, Mako Tok: Wright, van der Rohe, Nutra. But he had added his own touch by combining elements of industrial buildings and Japanese temples in each design. Of course, Ian hadn't known this before; his information was right out of the pages of the same *Architectural Digest* article where he had read about the grass.

Tok wanted his designs to be part of the landscape; he'd wanted them to be unexpected juxtapositions.

"Unexpected juxtapositions." Ian liked this phrase

"Did you say something?"

"No, just wondering where the agent is. It's kinda cool, isn't it, like a factory in the middle of a farm?"

Over the tick of the cooling engine was the muted roar of the happy chaotic family on the video getting up to some hijinks or other. The girls were still silent, maybe asleep, but no—she heard Chloe give a dry chuckle and Hannah her short bark of laughter.

"Ian, can we get out of the car? I'd really like to stretch my legs."

"Well the agent said we should wait for her before we start looking around. There's a particular way to approach the house in order to get what Tok termed 'the effect.'"

"Oh come on, Ian, more like *a*ffected. I'm getting out."

"I'll wait for the agent."

Emily held her peace. She knew what the house meant to Ian, the former geeky science kid, who had been what was indelicately termed a loser, for most of his young adult life. At thirty-five, that had begun to change with the start-up of his company and now at forty-five he was what Emily supposed was called a winner. She opened her door and stepped out of the car. The girls, taking their mother's cue, unbuckled their seatbelts and opened the side doors. Faintly she heard Ian ask them to wait but they slid out, stretching and yawning.

"Mom, why is Dad being so weird about this house?" Fifteen-year-old Chloe stood in front of her holding Paris, her Chihuahua in her arms. She was demanding and disgusted with everything, but Emily had to agree with her about the house.

Hannah, taking her big sister's cue, said, "Yeah, why is Daddy being so mean? It's an icky house. It's cold."

Hannah was right. Even in the dead middle of summer the area here in front of the house was cool. It must be the effect of the concrete, like a giant air conditioner. Tok's "effect." Emily snorted.

Hannah came over to her mother and wrapped Emily's arms around her like a blanket. "I'm cold, hold me." And Emily did, knowing that at the age of eight, the times when Hannah would voluntarily want to be hugged or touched would soon become fewer and fewer. Chloe submitted to any affectionate touch with a brittle resignation as if her impending adulthood would dissolve with any relaxation of vigilance.

There was a beep behind them. A silver Mercedes pulled up beside the Escalade and a woman in a pink Chanel suit got out. She was improbably tanned and her hair was waist-length blonde, expensively coloured and streaked. She couldn't have been a day under forty, but Botox gave her that indeterminate bland look that holds rich women in limbo between thirty and fifty.

Emily saw Ian's eyes as he got out of the car and shook hands with the real estate agent teetering in her Manolos, and wondered if he would be trading up wives too, now that he was a "winner."

The agent reached out and shook Emily's hand. "Hi, I'm Katie, your agent. I'm so glad you waited before exploring the property. The house is stunning if approached the right way. Tok was a genius."

"And if approached the wrong way?"

The real estate agent tilted her head and gave a veneered smile.

"Emily," Ian warned.

Emily threw up her hands in surrender and the agent gave a light, tinkling laugh. Ian turned to look at the agent again, his gaze caressing the quilted Chanel bag that hung from her shoulder.

Emily followed Ian and the agent up the path to the front door, the girls trailing behind. On either side of the path were stones, perfectly polished, rounded edges, no chips or pebbles, and then just grass, the flat lawn stretching endlessly beyond. No plants in pots, no small trees, not even those weird cactus things that so many landscape designers liked to use around modern houses. Just that perfectly mowed grass.

They path came to an end under the overhang of the concrete box that was supported by the blue pillars. Emily had a sudden vision of it falling and crushing them all. The girls shuffled behind them and Paris the Chihuahua yipped once.

The agent got the key out of the lock box and used it in the massive teak front door. There were two long narrow panes of glass on either side, running from the top to the bottom of the entranceway, but Emily thought that there still wouldn't be very much light, with only those thin windows and the overhang.

Emily was right. The entrance hall was dark and narrow, with rough concrete walls. There appeared to be wooden sconces set high up on the walls, but the agent didn't turn them on.

"Follow me," she said and trotted down the hall.

"Is there a hall closet?" Emily asked. She was ignored by Ian and the agent, but she felt Hannah's hand slip into hers.

"The Great Room," the agent said, sliding apart two doors on tracks. The doors slid back into the walls, and they all stood on the threshold of the Great Room, staring into more darkness.

"Damn, who closed those blinds?" The agent

stood there for a second, and Emily could almost feel her perkiness fading, but she soon got going again. "Wait here a second, folks. The last agent must have lowered the shades. They're hung from teak valances and are made of several layers of Japanese paper." She took off into the dim room. Emily smiled as she heard a short expletive every time the agent bumped into some architectural detail, but then she finally got the blinds up, one after another.

They gasped.

Sunlight flooded the room and the windows framed a panoramic view of the patchwork grasslands around the house.

But just as the blinds were opening, Emily could have sworn she saw someone slip through a doorway at the far end of the room. Just a quick blur, caught out of the corner of her eye. She shook her head. More "Tok effect."

"Mom, who was that?" Hannah whispered.

"Who?" She whispered back.

"That man that just went through that door?"

"Oh, that was just a shadow, honey."

Emily saw Chloe give them a sharp look, then bend her head over Paris. Ian and the agent were at the windows looking out over the land surrounding the house.

"Yes, it all belongs to the estate," the agent said, answering Ian's question.

"Who takes care of it?" Emily asked as she walked up to join them.

The agent looked blank. "I'm not sure. There's probably a number for the service back at the office." She rubbed her hands together. "Now the Family Room." She slid back two more doors, and again they looked into a dark room. This time the agent didn't swear, just opened the blinds. The rush of sunlight made them all blink. Instead of grasslands, they were looking at a pool set flush with the ground, a flat ledge of concrete separating it from the green expanse.

"A pool." Chloe put Paris down and walked over to the windows. Hannah followed her and all of them stood looking out, except Emily. Chloe turned and looked over her shoulder at her. "Mom, can I have a pool party?"

Somewhere in the house Emily thought she heard the faraway sound of a door closing. No one else seemed to notice.

They took the rest of the tour. Room after room: a kitchen full of industrial stainless steel appliances, a sunroom with hundreds of panes of glass separated only by black steel framing. "Safety glass," the agent assured her, Paris's nails skittering across hardwood, tiles, more concrete; no carpets in this house.

"Is that dog house-trained?" the agent asked Chloe after Paris disappeared around the corner of the kitchen. Chloe just eyed the agent with disdain, and Emily fell in love with her daughter all over again.

Ian said, "Of course, of course," and told Chloe to call Paris. He turned to the agent again and asked about the year the house was built and who had owned it last.

"A famous rock musician. Well, not famous like a front man; he was a songwriter and producer. Big, like Phil Spector. Huge in the eighties. Commissioned this house from Tok in 1982." The agent smiled at Ian and he smiled right back.

"What happened to the musician?" Chloe asked.

"Oh," the agent waved her hand vaguely, "he died."

Upstairs Emily heard Paris yelp, then they heard her little nails clicking frantically as she hurried back downstairs. The dog swept into the kitchen shivering, but she was a Chihuahua, and Chihuahuas always shivered. Chloe scooped her up and she peeked out from Chloe's arms with her bright black eyes as if to ask, *Can we go now?*

Emily knew how she felt.

2

When the moving van parked in front of the house, Emily said, "Our furniture is going to look lost in here."

"We'll buy more, we'll buy more," Ian said, bouncing on his toes.

"It's an hour from the city! I'm going to need a car to be able to see my friends." Chloe said, holding Paris to her chest and looking mournful.

"Next purchase, next purchase," Ian said, expansively putting an arm around her shoulders and squeezing.

Hannah just stood in the middle of the Great Room, sucking her finger and staring at the massive concrete fireplace against the wall.

The blinds were closed again. Emily supposed that now they had bought the house, they didn't need to be wooed with any special "effect." She walked over to the windows and opened the blinds. Sunlight filled the room like before. When she looked out the window she saw a man disappear under the overhang of the house, only catching a glimpse of his bent head and back. He was wearing grey.

"Ian, you better go talk to the movers, one of them has gone round back by mistake."

Their furniture rattled in the house's rooms. The arts-and-crafts wood pieces and the battered leather sofa barely made a dent in the Great Room. Their books filled only one of the floor-to-ceiling shelves in the Library, and Ian's desk disappeared into a corner of it. Her wicker chairs and table sat in the Sunroom looking like dancers come early to an empty ballroom. They hadn't been poor before, but this was living on a scale that Emily had no real conception of. She had an urge to gather all the furniture around the fireplace in the Great Room and live only there.

Ian was excited. He had visions of huge stainless steel tables, big important late-twentieth-century pieces, custom-made this and that. He showed Emily pictures of the house when the musician had owned it. Great expanses of floor broken by white fur rugs and big fibreglass pop art sculptures, white and red oversized leather pieces, glass tables balanced on slabs of concrete; all, Emily thought, absolutely horrible.

When it came time to parcel out the bedrooms in the house, Hannah wanted to share a room with Chloe.

"These bedrooms are too big. There's a man on the ceiling staring at me in that room." Hannah pointed to the room Emily had chosen for her. She looked up at Emily with teary eyes. "I want to share a room with Chloe."

Chloe, who had chosen her own room, one with a private bath and walk-in closet, put the kibosh on that, predictably enough.

"That little twit is not sharing a room with me. Besides, she makes Paris nervous."

"Chloe, don't call your sister a twit. And how the hell you can tell that dog is nervous, when all it does is shake all day long, is beyond me." Emily thought for a moment.

"Okay love, why don't you choose a room you like better?"

Hannah took Emily's hand. She said, "I like my old room, I want to go home," and the tears that had been threatening all day spilled down Hannah's miserable face. Emily, who was feeling much the same way at this point, gave her a hug.

"Look, sweetie, here on the other side of Chloe's bathroom is a nice little room just for you." Chloe sighed dramatically. Emily shot her a look and, mumbling to Paris, Chloe stomped off downstairs.

Hannah walked into the room cautiously, but then seemed to relax. "It's okay. But could we paint the wall pink?" She pointed to a wall of teak panels.

Emily laughed, imagining the look on Ian's face when presented with his daughter's decorating suggestions, and said, "We'll have to ask Daddy about that. But tell you what, we can get a hot pink furry rug."

Hannah jumped up and down: "When? When? When?"

Emily said, "Tomorrow."

When Ian heard about the pink rug at dinner that night, he looked apoplectic. "Maybe a nice antique kilim would be a better choice."

"I hate this house! And I hate *you*!" Hannah broke into tears again and Emily had to take her away from the dinner table and comfort her by rocking with her in the rocker for a while. After that, Ian acquiesced with bad grace.

That night in bed Emily said to him, "Ian, you're not the only one who has to live in this house."

Ian had wanted to go shopping for the proper sort of furniture he felt the house deserved, but he had been called back to work a few days after they bought the house, even though he had booked a week off. An hour's drive into the city and back didn't leave much time for shopping, and he absolutely refused to let Emily go without him, not even to pick up a few small things. Everything was to be subject to Ian's approval. So the rooms had remained largely empty.

"This place is cold enough, Ian, without making the kids live in Tok-effect bedrooms until you have the time to pick out furniture you think is up to his standards."

"They have to learn good taste sometime, Emily.

We can't indulge them in cheap throwaway culture forever."

"Since when," Emily asked, trying not to be as nasty as she wanted to be, "have you been an arbiter of taste? I seem to remember someone who held on to his *Star Trek* model ship until, well, until we moved."

Ian turned over in a huff. Emily turned off the light and listened to the house settle around them.

From the first, Emily had woken up in the mornings with bad dreams she couldn't quite remember, lingering like wisps of fog around the bedroom. Today was no different. She went downstairs, opened the blinds that always seemed to be closed and let light into the empty rooms.

Ian must close them in the night, she thought.

She had heard him walking around the house after they had gone to bed and she was only half awake, sinking into the middle of some dream. The girls joined her for breakfast around the stainless steel centre island in the kitchen and afterwards wandered off, Chloe to sit beside the pool, Paris at her heels, and Hannah to the Family Room, where she watched movies or played with Barbies close to the window where she could see Chloe.

We all seem drugged, Emily thought as she loaded

the dishwasher. *The girls haven't raised their voices once since we moved in, or asked to go to the mall, or to have friends over . . . and that dog.* Emily thought of Paris trotting after Chloe, nails click-clacking, its little head turning side to side in rapid, fearful sweeps. *I'll have to take it to the vet; it's off its food.*

Emily looked up from loading the dishwasher and, reflected in the black onyx behind it, she saw someone standing in the kitchen doorway.

"Hannah?" she asked, turning, but she knew it wasn't Hannah; the person had been too tall. She leaned against the counter and stared at the empty doorway. "You are definitely suffering from stress, Emily Masters," she said out loud, stopping when she realized she was just trying to fill the silent kitchen with noise.

In the Family Room, Hannah tired of watching *Cheaper by the Dozen* for the fifteenth time, and looked out the window to see where Chloe was. Chloe wasn't at the pool, but her towel was lying there beside it like a white bird lying flat on the concrete. Dead, like the bird that had flown into the window at home, the bird that she and Daddy had buried in the back garden. A burp of panic rose in her chest and she skittered into the Great Room where the blinds were closed again.

In the half-light, the open hearth of the fireplace

looked like a mouth, an open mouth asking her to walk in, to look and see what was up the chimney, waiting there in the dark. Hannah stood frozen.

That night, after Emily put a hysterical Hannah to bed, who kept insisting there was a man crouching in the Great Room fireplace, she confronted Ian again as they lay in bed.

"It's these empty rooms, Ian, even I find them spooky and I'm not ten years old. Why don't we hire a decorator?"

Ian looked at her with disbelief, "I *have* hired a decorator. Did you think I was going to furnish a place like this without professional advice? But it has to wait until I can go to the auctions in the fall. Meanwhile, she's keeping a lookout for some important pieces."

"How about some unimportant pieces? Why can't we just order something online?"

"Emily, you know nothing about it. You don't even appreciate the house you're living in."

Emily looked at Ian and had a flash of insight. "Ian, who is this decorator?"

To his credit, Ian did look a little flustered. "Well, you met her—the agent, Katie. Her full name's Katie Eisen. She's a very well-respected interior designer. Her work has been in *Architectural Digest*." He stopped and looked at Emily and she saw the excitement rising in his eyes. "In fact, Katie says when she finishes with the house, we might get a spread in the magazine. Can you imagine?"

"Oh, I can imagine very well."

"What's that supposed . . . ?" but before Ian could finish, the house rocked with a loud bang, as if something heavy had fallen over downstairs.

"What the hell? Did that dog knock something over? I told Chloe to keep it in her room, its claws will ruin the surface of the floors."

"It *is* in her room, Ian. Besides, Paris couldn't make that much noise."

Emily and Ian climbed out of bed. Emily tied her robe around her and Ian fumbled for his slippers. The girls were running down the hall, Paris clutched tightly in Chloe's arms.

"Mommy." Hannah ran to her and hugged her around her waist. With a pang Emily saw her lips and eyes were still swollen from her tears that afternoon. Chloe's eyes were very wide; she looked younger with her hair pulled back into a ponytail.

"Girls, go back to bed. Your father and I will go down and see what happened."

Chloe spoke, her voice trembling, "You're not leaving us up here alone."

Ian waved at them to be quiet and started down the dark hall to the stairs; they followed him, keeping close together.

Like lemmings, Emily thought, then pushed the image out of her mind.

"Why don't we just call the police?" Chloe whispered to her mother as they snuck down the stairs in the dark.

Why indeed, Emily thought. Because Ian was a man, and calling in outside help this early in the game was a sign of weakness? But she hadn't thought of the police either, until Chloe mentioned it.

"I've got my cell." Chloe whispered when they stood outside the kitchen. The house was silent except for the shuffling and breathing of their little group. Ian put his finger to his lips and went into the kitchen. They all followed. Emily heard Hannah's breath coming in hitching little gasps. She was hanging off of Emily's hand and her fingers were icy. Ian took a big kitchen knife from the rack on the wall and entered the Family Room. They came up a little behind him, Emily a bit stunned at the sight of Ian with the big knife held tight in his fist. She realized he was enjoying this display of ownership, of defending his property.

The room was dark and empty. Ian pushed open the sliding doors to the Great Room and Hannah whimpered beside Emily. He tiptoed in and it was dark in there too; of course the blinds were closed. Emily knew there was no one in the house. Ian was just playing Cowboys and Indians. She walked over and switched on the lights. From wooden sconces around the room, light poured yellow up the walls. Their lonely furniture looked deserted in the huge room.

"Why the hell did you do that? Someone could be in one of the other rooms." But Ian spoke in a normal voice and put the knife down on a coffee table.

"Because there is no one in here and you know it." She walked over to the blinds and pulled them open with a hard tug. "And why the hell do you keep closing the damn blinds every night? Some 'Tok effect'?"

"I've never touched those blinds, not once since we've moved in here," Ian yelled, his face red with anger.

Hannah burst into tears and Paris began to howl.

3

Emily and the girls went out in her Volvo the next day. In the city they bought a bright pink fun-fur rug, a purple vinyl beanbag chair, and ordered a bed and dresser from Pottery Barn Kids for Hannah's room. Then they bought a sleigh bed that Chloe wanted and arranged to have it delivered, along with a dresser and a big blue and yellow oriental rug for her bedroom. Emily filled the car with plants for the Sunroom and a few more pieces of wicker. She wanted to go further and just order furniture for all the rooms at the ordinary furniture stores, with maybe a few Ikea trips thrown in, but she knew Ian would be furious. It was only because the girls' rooms were out of sight that she even took a chance on furnishing them without his input. Ian had left that morning, a little subdued, but defiant.

The boyishness that had attracted her to Ian in the first place had, with his success, somehow become greed instead of lightheartedness. Emily wondered if being the butt of jokes for most of your school life, never getting the girl in your twenties, froze you in some sort of boyhood limbo, so that no matter how many goodies you got later in life, it was never enough. Emily thought about all this as she set up her computer on a wicker desk in the Sunroom, which was now half-filled with plants. It was a start. At least this room was bright, and didn't have those goddamn blinds. Emily would love to rip them all down. Whatever happened to curtains? She would insist the blinds go.

She saw a man in grey standing beside the swimming pool, staring down into it, but she ignored him. If the house had a ghost, so be it. When she looked up again, he was gone.

She Googled Mako Tok. There were pictures of his buildings, too sterile for Emily's taste, and pictures of him at glittering parties. Handsome, dark, wearing suits and over-designed glasses, his arm usually around the shoulders of some blonde that looked much like their agent, Katie. Critical acclaim, fame, the office tower in New York, the museum in Spain, the private houses for celebrities, Emily scrolled through web entry after web entry.

What Katie hadn't told them, though Emily suspected that Ian knew, was that Tok's final commission had been a monastic retreat in the desert for Jesuit brothers. He had designed one of his most acclaimed buildings, all white and spare. It stood out on the desert landscape like an iceberg.

In the brothers' chapel he had used white onyx, and there, in that perfect, empty, serene room he had blown his brains out the day before the grand opening. Of course, the details weren't in the regular news pieces, but there was something of a Mako Tok cult online, and there were sites dedicated just to him.

These sites had plenty of information, including the fact that they had had to totally redo the white birch floor in the chapel because the bloodstains wouldn't come out. There was even a picture of the chapel with a man face down and a dark stain spreading across the floor under him. The site, www. TokAboutIt.com, claimed it was a real picture of the crime scene, taken by one of the investigators. It made Emily sick to look at it, but she told herself it could have been Photoshopped by any obsessive, pimply teenager with the right program. Another article said the Jesuit brothers only used the retreat for a year before selling it to a company that turned it into a high-priced spa, Desert Wind Retreat. The spa was very popular with movie stars.

They had dinner together at the old dining room table in the Family Room that night. The Dining Room of the house hadn't been used once since they moved in because there was no furniture in it.

Ian's good mood was back, so Emily risked a question. "Ian, do you think we could take those blinds down?"

Ian looked at her likes she was crazy. "Those blinds are the work of a twentieth-century master. They are integral to the design and the spirit of the house."

"Ian, they won't stay open. This place is dark as a tomb."

"I'll get someone in to fix it." He took a stab at his lasagne. "You'll feel better when there's some furniture in here. Katie has found some wonderful pieces for us. I was thinking you and I could go to the city tomorrow, look at the furniture and spend the night. Sort of a weekend retreat." Ian took Emily's hand and she knew he was trying to make up with her.

"I wouldn't feel comfortable here on my own," Chloe said, Paris shivering on her lap.

"The dog should not be up at the table." Ian shook his finger at her. "Oh, you're good, you're very good. I'll pay you for your babysitting time. How much do you get an hour these days?"

"It's not that."

"I'll stay here, Ian. You go and look at the furniture with Katie," Emily said.

"Are you sure? Chloe could take a little responsibility." But even as he said it, Emily saw that this was what he had really wanted, not a weekend away with her.

"I'm sure." She pulled her hand out from under his and patted it. "Ian, who has been looking after the grass?"

"The grass?"

"Yes, has a service been here?"

"The grass is perfect, it looks fine to me. Maybe Katie called them." Ian blushed and looked down at his plate, then took a bite of his salad.

"Probably." Emily said and took a sip of wine. Somewhere in the house there was the sound of a heavy piece of furniture shifting. They all ignored it.

Emily dreamt about the musician. She still didn't know his name in waking life. She had Googled Tok's clients, but they weren't all listed. He had been discreet about his commissions. She had looked up eighties musicians and music producers, but she recognized the faces of most from record albums and music videos. If she didn't recognize them, she dug deeper, but there was never any specific mention of where they lived, just the country, or sometimes the city. Apparently the public didn't really care where the men behind the music called home.

In her dream he was blond and blue-eyed. Arrogant. He wore a grey suit and a white shirt with an open collar. She was sitting at her desk in the Sunroom and he was leaning against the doorway.

"You like my house?" His smile was sardonic, as if he, like Ian, doubted she could appreciate the place.

"It's our house, and no, not particularly." Emily wasn't scared, only a little impatient with this intruder.

"Are you kidding? I commissioned this house; it was designed to my specifications. It is the outward expression of me." He crossed his arms and smiled at her, a smile that was not reflected in his eyes.

"You mean cold and dated? We've decided to ignore you." Emily pinched a dead leaf off one of her plants. In her dream, the Sunroom was completely filled with greenery. The musician stopped smiling.

"Maybe I'll make you pay attention. Maybe you've ignored me for too long. Should have got rid of me when you had the chance. Now I'm here to stay." The musician took a step toward her and Emily felt something warm running down her hand. She looked at it and saw that the leaf she had pinched was bleeding. Streams of blood flowed between her fingers and spread across the white birch floor. He grabbed her wrist and pulled her close to him.

"Have you been in the Music Room yet?" She looked at him and it was Mako Tok, his face blown away, only a mass of bloody pulp moving and speaking to her. "Have you been in the Music Room yet?"

Emily woke up with a start. From far away in the house came the brief jangle of piano keys. She edged closer to Ian, who slept, his mouth slightly open—dreaming, she knew, of his important late-twentieth-century pieces and Katie lying nude among them.

4

After Ian left in the morning, waving to them from the white Escalade with a grin on his face, the girls sat in the Family Room playing video games and Emily got online again. In the Sunroom, with its grey slate floor, not white birch as in the dream, she Googled musicians, Tok, eighties musicians, blond musicians again, but nowhere could she find a connection between the house and any of the celebrities, minor or otherwise.

She made them all chicken and rice for dinner. They ate around the kitchen island. With Ian gone, the girls seemed to relax a little, as if he had been the reason for the stress in the house. Even Paris was in a good mood, eating bites of chicken that Chloe held out for her and yapping whenever the conversation got loud. After dinner they sat on the sofa in front of the TV and watched a video, not *Cheaper by the Dozen*, like Hannah begged, but *Yours, Mine & Ours*, the new one with Renee Russo, which was just as bad, Emily privately thought.

While they watched, sharing popcorn out of the big ceramic bowl, he came to the doorway of the Family Room. Emily didn't turn her head. Neither did the girls, but Hannah whispered, "He's there, Mom."

"Ignore him." Emily said, but with a little shiver, she remembered her dream. He stood for a moment longer, then turned away. They heard the blinds slide closed in the Great Room. They heard him walking heavily through the house, moving furniture. Once there was a crash like glass breaking, then the sound of a piano. The blinds in the Family Room closed and both girls screamed. Emily stood up.

"Right." She walked over to the blinds and pulled them open. Early evening sun filled the room again, but then—slowly, inexorably—the blinds inched downwards. She grabbed a blind as high up as she could and pulled, but it wouldn't come down. She hung on it with all her weight, until there was a snapping sound. The blind pulled away, paper and splintered wood scattering the floor. She kept tugging until the entire blind was down. She tore at the other four windows, the girls getting into the act. Sometimes the blinds would not come away completely, but hung, ripped and broken from the valances, but at least the light could come in, at least they could no longer open and close.

They moved into the Great Room, Emily turning on all the lights, and started to tear down the blinds. From the other rooms there was the sound of suppressed fury, the indistinct roar of someone yelling. Emily smiled and thought that was how Ian would sound when he came back and found they had destroyed his precious blinds.

They tore and tore, late into the night, Paris yapping at their feet. The sounds in the house had stopped; the only noise was their shouting and laughter as they ripped the heavy paper down and let in the moonlight.

Finally, Emily sent the girls to bed exhausted, their hands bleeding where the heavy paper and splinters of wood had cut them. Her own hands were bloody and sore and as she stood in the bathroom washing them, she wondered what had come over them. Ian would be furious. The soap stung the cuts as Emily watched the pinkish water swirl down the drain under the running taps. She glanced up in the mirror and he was there behind her.

He was not smiling.

"I kept the blinds closed to preserve the art, the priceless furniture. You've ruined it. You appreciate nothing." As Emily turned and stood with her back against the sink, she saw a small trickle of blood start to run from behind his ear onto the shoulder of his grey suit. "At least you didn't touch the Music Room." He turned and walked away. Emily saw now that the side of his head was blown away, the blond hair blackened and encrusted with blood around a gaping hole.

The Music Room. It must be one of the rooms they hadn't gotten to. Emily knew he would leave only when that room was torn open as well. She hurried down the stairs. She couldn't remember which room Katie had called the Music Room. She thought it was at the front of the house, the one right off the front hall, if you turned the other way instead of going into the Great Room.

She stood in front of its brushed steel door, her heart pounding. The knob turned easily in her hand. The room was predictably big and empty, the main difference being there *were* no windows, only walls which looked like they were padded, covered in some sort of white fabric. For the sound, Emily realized— no sound could enter or leave this room. The floor was white birch and there was a stain in the centre of it. She edged back toward the door. Without scissors or a knife there was nothing she could do in here, the walls would be impervious to her fingers.

With a thunk, the door swung shut.

Emily wasn't really worried; a little scared of course, but really, what could the ending of this story be? He was dead, a ghost. A bit poltergeisty perhaps, but it wasn't like she was in an abusive relationship with the guy or anything.

His voice licked her ear: "My name is Sebastian Cole." Her hand found the doorknob and she turned it. The door opened and she slipped out.

5

She didn't Google him the next morning. She didn't care how he died, or what his story was. From the back of his head she had a pretty good idea what the answer to that was. Emily refused to enter into a relationship with this ghost whose behaviour reminded her so much of her husband's. In fact, she thought, as her scissors tore through the fabric on the Music Room walls, that probably *was* his story. Sebastian Cole, band geek made good, but still always in the background, still a little resentful of what the other boys had, and seeing women as the enemies who had laughed in his face when he asked them out at age sixteen. The padding behind the fabric came out in big drifts, catching in her hair and skidding across the floor. She had propped the door open with a heavy chair and the girls stood in the doorway watching her. Paris ran into the room and jumped around in the cottony insulation, yapping happily.

"Daddy's going to kill you," Hannah said.

"No he won't," Emily said, ripping through another panel, although she wasn't so sure.

"Are you sure you shouldn't be wearing some kind of mask? Is that stuff safe?" Chloe asked.

"Perfectly," Emily said, though she wasn't sure about that either. Maybe it was full of poisonous little fibres that would catch in her lungs and kill her with cancer. Then the ghost would have the last laugh. "Why don't you guys tear down the rest of the blinds?"

"Cool," Hannah said. She and Chloe hurried down the hall, Paris at their heels. Emily heard them laughing and shouting as the rest of the blinds were ripped from their valance. The house had lost its repressive quality, despite Sebastian Cole possibly still lurking around somewhere. There was no stain in the middle of the floor either, that had been a trick of the light last night, or a hallucination.

Emily could almost feel Sebastian fade with every handful of acoustic paneling she destroyed. When she reached the last stretch of padding, Emily found a slit in one of the panels. She stuck her hand in and came out with a sheaf of Polaroids. Close-ups of Sebastian Cole, smiling disdainfully at whoever was holding the camera. Sebastian holding a gun to his head. To Emily it looked as if he was showing off. The last picture was of Sebastian face down on the floor in the Music Room, a dark stain spreading beneath him. Were the photos real? Or staged? Emily couldn't tell. She ripped them up and added them to the drifts of padding and fabric covering the floor.

When she finished the last of the walls, she swept the litter into a black plastic bag. This room could be two nice coat closets and a powder room.

She heard the Escalade come up the drive. Still holding the broom, she came out into the front hall. Here the floor was still littered with padding and fabric. The girls came to the doorway of the Great Room, and then when they heard the key in the front door, joined their mother in the hall, standing on either side of her. Chloe held Paris still, shushing her when she yapped at the sound of Ian's voice. Hannah took her mother's hand. The three of them walked out onto the pathway in front of the house.

Ian was holding a lamp that Emily supposed was an important piece of twentieth-century design. Just over his shoulder, Emily could see Katie, carrying a truly ugly piece of sculpture. They stopped. Ian looked at Emily, her hair full of batting; he pushed past her, still carrying the lamp, and stood in the doorway of the Great Room. Emily knew she had ruined the "Tok effect." The three of them turned to watch Ian go into the house. He came to the front door, his face scarlet, holding the lamp in his fist like a weapon. Katie spun on her Christian Louboutin heel and fled to the Escalade, the sculpture clutched to her chest.

"What the hell have you done to my house?" Ian roared.

Hannah's hand tightened on hers.

"Not your house, Ian," Emily said, unsmiling, bending down to pull out a weed that had sprouted between the walkway edges. "Ours."

When Emily straightened up again she saw Sebastian Cole standing beside Ian. The looks of outrage on their faces were identical. Then, shaking his head in disgust, Sebastian Cole began to fade, giving her one last wounded look before he disappeared permanently.

Ian lowered the lamp he had been holding like some medieval lord wielding a mace against marauding peasants and slumped down on the front door step.

"All I wanted was a nice house."

Emily sat down beside him and put her arm around his shoulders. "I know, Ian. And you will have a nice house, and you have a nice family to live in it with you." She picked up the lamp and inspected it closely. "Ian, do you even really like this stuff?"

Ian looked at the lamp as if he had never seen it before. "Not really, no." He gazed around at the grounds and the house, the girls chasing Paris over the flat grass and turned back to Emily.

"Emily, do you think maybe we could put in a rock-climbing wall? I've always wanted one of those."

Emily nodded and said, "Sure thing. But Hannah gets to paint her walls pink."

Ian didn't even flinch, just took Emily's hand in his.

The Other Door

She had travelled halfway across the world, and it was only on the rattling train into Paris that she felt it was finally over. Even the old man begging, whose eyes, milky and crusted, seemed to linger on her a moment too long when she waved him away, didn't bother her. Here he was just another unfortunate human, not a portent of anything, anything at all.

The apartment she had rented in Paris was perfect. Located in the 14th arrondissement in an old Paris building with a courtyard and a concierge, it was enough of a cliché to make her self-conscious. Just outside the door were bistros and boulangeries, fromageries and bookstalls.

The apartment itself was made up of two airy rooms with floor-to-ceiling French windows in the dining and living area. Outside the windows were small, black wrought iron balconies. Mia instantly had visions of herself leaning over them in the mornings, croissant and café au lait in hand, watching Parisians as they went about being, well, Parisians. She wandered all around the apartment looking into every corner and cupboard, the tiny kitchen, the small bathroom, like a cat in a strange place.

Mia opened the bedroom window to let the street noises in and sat down in the armchair beside it. In that rush of ordinary noises she seemed to hear the words, *everything's fine, everything's fine*, like a soothing lullaby a mother would use to lull her restless child to sleep. She sat there, listening for hours as the afternoon shadows lengthened without her noticing. Now that it was over and she was away from Him, she could think logically; she could make some plans as to what to do. She had all the time in the world to clean the taint of Him from her; for now she could just sit. When the room had darkened almost completely, she came back to herself. Looking up she could see, next to the wardrobe that took up most of one wall, a door. Had it been there before? Of course it had been. She just hadn't noticed in her relief at arriving. The door had no handle. Someone had removed the hardware.

Mia got up and put her hand against the white-painted wood of the door. It was cool. There was no light coming through the hole where the handle had been. She pushed against the door and it gave slightly, but didn't open. Mia had to almost physically fight the urge to bend down and put her eye to the keyhole.

You're being stupid; it's just an old closet they closed up. Vaguely troubled, Mia left the bedroom.

That night Mia ate in. She had gone out in the early evening and bought some groceries. Now she sat at the wooden table with the Provençal cloth, eating and flipping through her Paris guidebook. In the living area there was a tile fireplace; it had once been gas, but now was unused.

It's really too bad, she thought, looking at the empty grate—contrary to the romantic vision of Paris in April, it was rainy and cold outside. The sky was a bleak grey turning to sodden black in the evening, with massed clouds that moved like a living creature above the city.

Mia watched the lamplight play over the ceramic lions that guarded the arch of the fireplace box— their mouths open in a silent roar. The interlocking shadows and light made it look as if their eyes shone and then dimmed as they contemplated her. Occasionally, air would rush down the chimney and the fireplace would sigh, as if the lions were trying to whisper. Mia wasn't afraid. They were just a turn-of-the-century fancy, useless now without the fire that they had guarded. Now that she was away from Him, everything had fallen back into its proper place.

Still jet-lagged, Mia could barely keep her eyes open. She cleared away the dishes she had used and stumbled through preparations for bed. She collapsed on the bed and pulled the duvet up to her chin, wrapping herself in its feathery depths.

This is a good place, was her last thought before she fell deeply asleep.

He came again in her dreams, and His eye was inexorable and His face was kind at first, but Mia resisted. The dog was there too, sighing at her feet, whispering in and about the leaves on the ground—only when he looked up, he had the face of a lion. She could see the blood again, and the place in the woods, only this time something moved beneath the leaves. And there was the centipede on the floor of the shower, its legs like the eyelashes of some giant eye that twitched in its sleep as it dreamt . . . what? She didn't know, she didn't know—and Mia snapped awake.

Light from the street lamps didn't fall far from the window, so the brunt of the room was in the dark. Mia lay there, heart pounding. From behind the other door came a scrambling. She turned on her side to face the door and it stopped. She lay there as still as possible and in a minute the noise started up again. She heard the old dragging sound, that sound she thought she had finished with forever and then that stopped too.

He can't be here. Her heart would not stop its noisy

beating; she could see it in her mind's eye, ruby and pulsing, calling Him. Mia watched the door, sure that it would open, sure that it would reveal its secret. But nothing happened. The pull was so strong she couldn't bear it. She turned on the bedside light and swung her legs out of bed. She crept across the floor to the door, as if He wouldn't hear whatever she did. She touched the door with her hand—it was a plain ordinary painted wood door, nothing here to be frightened of. She got on her knees in front of it, like a supplicant waiting for Communion, and slowly brought her eye to the keyhole. Nothing. She laid her ear on the door right next to the place where the handle had been removed.

Then she heard it, and from the black holes in the wood the centipede ran, its legs scuttling soft, right into her screaming mouth.

An Unexpected Thing

He woke up with one of his wife's hairs caught between his teeth. He knew it was hers because the baby had hardly any hair on her head yet and his mistress Diana had short black hair. The hair caught in his teeth was long. He could feel it curling around whenever he touched it with his tongue. Lying in bed he worried at it, trying to get it out by pulling at it, but the hair wouldn't budge. Next to him, his wife Miranda slept soundly, her long pale brown hair, the same hair that was currently wound around his tooth, spread across her pillow. For one vicious moment he imagined taking a knife and sawing away at that hair so that she would be shorn and never again would her hair be in his mouth.

As if she had heard his thoughts, his wife turned over and opened her cornflower-blue eyes. "Hello darling," she said, yawning, showing her little white cat teeth. "Did you sleep well?"

Guy grimaced at his wife, used to exaggerating his tired state so that she would not expect too much of him in the coming day. "Not so well, and now I have a goddamn hair caught in my teeth."

"Oh," she said sitting up. "Poor baby. Go brush your teeth, I'm sure it will come out."

"What a good idea," Guy said. "I don't know why I didn't think of it myself."

"Oh, stop being such an old grouch. I'll make coffee."

Why don't you brush your teeth. Of course I was going to brush my teeth, how else would I get the hair out, you moron? Guy opened his mouth wide in the mirror. His tongue was a little coated and he thought his throat might be a bit red. He got close to the mirror and looked for the hair. He could feel it with his tongue, it was driving him crazy, but he couldn't see it.

He brushed vigorously and flossed for good measure, baring his pearly whites in a toothy smile. *Looking good, Guy.* He felt much better. In the shower he soaped his body vigorously and roared out a song.

Miranda heard Guy singing, even down in the kitchen. She hoped he wouldn't wake Isabelle, the baby's howling and immediate demands were not something she wanted to add to the general morning chaos, not until Guy's overripe ass in his blue Italian suit was out the door for the day. She threw some kibble in Kitty Cat's dish and foamed the milk for Guy's latte. Miranda poured her own cup of coffee and stirred in two teaspoons of sugar, then sat at the table and watched Kitty Cat enjoy her breakfast.

The cat, a black and white she-cat they had rescued from the Humane Society, would delicately choose a piece of kibble from the bowl and then move it to the back of her jaw where she would crunch it between her sharp teeth, tilting her head to the side and squinting her eyes in concentration. Miranda wondered if Kitty Cat was imagining crushing the hard little skulls of mice between her teeth when they closed on the kibble, if that was the reason for her apparent relish of such a dull food.

Miranda took a sip of her coffee and thought about her day ahead—she really wanted a chance to try that new recipe, but first she would take the baby to "Mommy and Me" at the community centre, and maybe if the weather stayed nice, work in the yard a bit. Isabelle could play on the blanket in the sun while Miranda tended to her plants. *Sounds like a plan.*

Kitty Cat looked up from her dish, her ears swivelling forward. Guy pounded down the stairs, the soles of his loafers slap-slapping on each stair as he came. Kitty Cat left her breakfast and leapt into Miranda's lap. She didn't like Guy particularly, regarded him with a wary eye. Guy was definitely a dog man. In fact he had been angling for some time for a Golden Retriever, or a Lab. Something big and bouncy. Miranda had pleaded for a grace period, at least until the baby was walking. She knew that despite Guy's enthusiasm, she was the one who would end up walking the dog.

Guy smiled at Miranda sitting at the kitchen table. She looked very pretty in her pink robe, with her light brown hair spilled across her shoulders. Very feminine. When he kissed her, he could smell her skin cream; it had the faint scent of flowers. He took a giant swig of his coffee. Miranda also made a mean latte.

"Well darling, I'm off. Going to make money to keep you in the style to which you have grown accustomed." He kissed her extravagantly, juggling his coffee cup in one hand and winding the other through her hair.

I wonder what Diana's up to. I should buy her a little gift, and have to remember to get more condoms. Tonight we should order in at her place, don't want to waste time going out for dinner. I'll have to be back by nine or Miranda will worry.

Miranda's voice broke through his thoughts.

". . . hair?"

"What hair?" Guy asked shrugging into his jacket, still shifting his coffee cup from hand to hand.

"The one you had caught in your teeth this

morning, silly. Is it still there or did you get it out?"

"Oh lord, I'd forgotten all about that. Out, it's out. I have to do some work at the office tonight, get these drawings out by tomorrow. So I'll probably be home latish, say nine?"

"You work way too hard, Guy."

Guy tossed his head, feeling very responsible and adult.

"Have a good day, darling," he said, opening the front door. "I'll see you tonight."

He slammed the door behind him. Miranda stared into her coffee cup, a little frown on her face. Upstairs, the baby began to cry.

Isabella really is a pretty baby, Miranda thought as she squeezed the baby's chubby little arms into her pink onesie and matching cardigan after Isabella had had her organic oatmeal and soymilk bottle. The baby bounced up and down on her pearly toes when Miranda stood her up to snap the crotch of the playsuit. She put the baby on her hip and ran her hand over Isabella's downy head, the small blonde duck-curl of hair that Miranda was already mourning. *If only*, Miranda thought, *babies weren't so goddamn boring*. Pretending to enjoy playing patty cake over and over was not her forte, but she did it with determination.

When she had first gotten pregnant, she had

imagined walking with Guy through the park, or to the neighbourhood coffee shop, the baby peering from a Snuggie strapped to Guy's chest while Miranda held his hand and gazed at them. Guy giving the baby a bottle late at night in the glow of the nightlight, while Miranda tiptoed in and watched from the shadows as Guy became a real father. The two of them bathing the baby in the plastic blue tub and wondering at this wonderful thing they had made and planning the future.

Of course none of that had come true. Guy had not even brought a bunch of flowers to the hospital after the birth. When they'd had friends over for dinner, Guy had said that the birth was the most disgusting thing he had ever seen. They'd all laughed like it was a joke, but Miranda felt the pity emanating off her friends.

No, there was no hope of rescue, she realized as she dutifully read *Goodnight Moon* to Isabella for the thirtieth time, even though Isabella would rather try to stuff her own foot in her mouth and gurgle. The two of them were in this alone. But Miranda did not have to like it.

Guy had a photo of Miranda and himself on his desk, a photo of Isabella in his wallet and a photo of his mistress on his computer. In the picture, Diana was wearing a fire-engine-red bikini and was holding some sort of tropical drink with an umbrella in it. Her skin was a lovely uniform golden brown and Guy knew there were no tan lines under the little scraps of fabric. The picture had been taken in the Bahamas that winter while Guy was at his in-laws over the Christmas holidays.

The message Diana had sent along with the photo was brief: *Having a wonderful time, glad you're not here. Cheers, Diana.* Guy didn't gaze at the picture obsessively or use it to masturbate at lunchtime with the office door securely locked—no, he wasn't that kind of dribbling fool. He just liked to know it was there—a reminder of the complexity of what seemed an outwardly simple life, an example of his own cleverness at being able to have his cake and eat it too.

Guy was very careful. He never paid for any of his evenings with Diana with a credit card—only cash and only from a private account that Miranda had no idea existed. He never bought gifts for the two of them from the same store; he didn't even shop for them in the same parts of town. He never took Diana anyplace that might remotely be a place any of the suburbanite mommies and their clean-cut husbands might frequent. Diana didn't mind. She liked smoky wine bars and little bistros, and eating Chinese food from the carton after sex. Guy was always careful to stay out no later than ten. Miranda had no cause for suspicion or complaint.

The "Mommy and Me" group was held in a library basement, a few blocks from where Miranda and Guy lived. In a brightly lit room with industrial blue carpet and sturdy climbing toys, battered books on low shelves and lots of primary-coloured cushions with suspicious stains lying on the floor, about seven babies at various stages of early childhood development crawled, lay on their backs or wiggled on their stomachs making futile swimming motions. Their mothers sat in a protective circle just outside them, as if they had tossed the babies into a particularly rich poker pot and the game was winner take all. All of the mothers, including Miranda, had been professional women once. Sylvia had been a doctor, Laura an ad exec, Evelyn . . .

Where was Evelyn today? Miranda wondered as she set Isabella down among the other babies.

Before they were pregnant all of these women had read *Cookie* magazine in line at the supermarket; they'd passed by Baby Gap on the weekend and wondered what photo-ready baby theirs would look like; they had cooed over strangers' babies at various events and listened avidly to friends' stories of their husbands' faces when they first saw their son or daughter. They had seen the baby in insurance ads and wanted to plan their future. During pregnancy they had read *What to Expect When You're Expecting* and cried during the movie the hospital Lamaze class showed of a baby being born naturally. They had been sold down the line.

"Miranda." Sarah—once a theatre director of some renown, now mother of Matthew and talking wistfully of starting a home jewellery business someday—leaned over and whispered in her ear. "Did you try that recipe?"

Miranda nodded. "Last night. I don't think it was much of a success though. Where's Evelyn today?"

"Didn't you hear about Evelyn? Alex died last night, in his sleep. They think it was a heart defect."

"Oh my God, really?"

Sarah nodded, bouncing Matthew on her knee.

"I'll have to call her."

"You should. I'm going to call her after the class. It must have been such a shock."

Before Miranda or Sarah could say anything more, the class leader, Sylvia—once a doctor, now mother of Hannah—clapped her hands. "Mommies, it's time to begin."

She reached into a plastic bin and began to pull out brightly coloured musical instruments. They were passed around the circle. Some women had rainbow-striped tambourines or little clackers made to look like green frogs, others had yellow horns shaped like ducks. Miranda was handed a pair of maracas that were cherry red and had little women dancing in flowing skirts on them. She laid Isabella down on the cushion in front of her. Some women held their babies on their laps, but most of them placed or sat their babies in front of them, on cushions.

The leader started them off.

Peter Peter pumpkin eater
Had a wife and couldn't keep her;
He put her in a pumpkin shell
And there he kept her very well.

All of the other women joined in, repeating the nursery rhyme and using the various musical instruments to keep a sort of broken time. There was always a little hesitancy at the beginning of the circle; the women felt self-conscious and a bit foolish. It was the babies that allowed them to go beyond this reaction and start to put some feeling into it. They were doing this for their children. By the third go round on "Peter Peter," they were surprisingly all on the same rhythm.

Then came:

Georgie Porgie pudding and pie,
Kissed the girls and made them cry.

When the boys came out to play,
Georgie Porgie ran away.

Miranda looked down at Isabella, who seemed entranced, watching her mother avidly.

Pat-a-cake, pat-a-cake Baker's man,
Bake me a cake as fast as you can;
Pat it and prick it and mark it with B,
And put it in the oven for Baby and me.

The rhymes went on endlessly; they wandered through "Goosey Goosey Gander," and "Ring Around the Rosie," "Three Blind Mice" and "Hark, Hark, the Dogs Do Bark." Miranda's maracas never faltered; they were a red blur next to her face, the little dancing lady goading her on. The words became nonsense; there was only Isabella and Miranda in the room, in the world. It seemed she remembered the rhymes segueing into—

Tell Tale Tit
Your tongue shall be slit
And all the dogs in town
Shall have a little bit.

The babies had fallen asleep, Isabella with her fist half in her mouth, but still the mommies went on. The colours in the room seemed to grow brighter and brighter, the animals in the posters on the wall came down and danced with them. Paddington Bear, the Very Hungry Caterpillar, Clifford the Big Red Dog. They looked more like beasts and less like anthropomorphized animals meant to entertain children. They danced in and out of the circle, brushing against the women, bringing their own animal smells to the room already ripe with the scents of sweat, milk, baby waste.

Finally, when Miranda felt she could take no more, that her mind would surely crack if one more rhyme came from her lips or the plastic band of childish instruments didn't stop, the leader called a halt.

Guy was signing the last contract of the day when he felt the hair again. *Goddamn it, thought I got the bugger out this morning. Unless it was that crappy place I had lunch. Probably some illegal immigrant's hair between my teeth, those bastards never use hairnets.*

He teased it with his tongue, feeling the thin stretch of it. Sticking his hand deep into his mouth, he tried to grab hold of it, but he couldn't pin down what teeth in the back it was stuck between. He wiggled his nail between his teeth, and only succeeded in scratching his gum. Finally he got up and went to the company bathroom. Staring into the mirror, he opened his mouth wide. He saw the hair, twined between his back molars. He tugged it upwards between the two teeth and it came out, but he almost gagged with the effort.

The fucker. Guy stared at the hair. It looked like another one of Miranda's, long and light-coloured. *That's it, she is getting her hair cut.* Guy rinsed his mouth out over and over again with handfuls of water. He'd brush his teeth at Diana's tonight.

On the way to pick up Diana, he stopped at a little corner convenience store. They had flowers in plastic buckets outside the entrance. He picked a bunch of pink gerbera daisies. They reminded him of Miranda, simple, feminine and pretty. He had the storekeeper wrap them in paper and paid the $8.99. He put them beside him on the seat of the car and drove the rest of the way to Diana's work, listening to 50 Cent on the CD player.

Diana had just locked up the high-end boutique she owned and was waiting for him outside, having a cigarette. The faceless mannequins in the window were dressed in various shades of red, their stylized arms reaching toward the glass, showing that their hands were handcuffed together. Around their skinny plaster ankles were balls and chains.

"Good God, Diana, what the hell is that?" Guy gestured to the display as Diana came over and leaned in his open window. Guy always liked it when she did that; it made him feel as if he were picking up a prostitute, being really hedonistic. It made the affair seem even dirtier than it was.

Diana turned her head to take in the window, and back to Guy. "Oh, my window dresser Simon came up with it. Slave to fashion and all that. I love it." She blew smoke out of the side of her mouth and smiled at Guy.

"Well I don't. It's creepy. It's more like BDSM or something."

"Oh, Guy." Diana cocked her head. "I didn't do it for you. Besides, what would you know about BDSM."

Guy didn't like being made to feel straitlaced. "Are you going to get in the car or what?"

Diana ground her cigarette out under the heel of her stiletto pump. "I might not, if you're going to be so snarky."

"Sorry, sorry." Guy sighed. "It's just been a bitch of a day and Miranda will want me home about nine. You know how I hate to rush my time with you."

Diana walked around the Mercedes and opened the door. She picked up the flowers on the seat and slid in. "Oh, flowers. How . . . nice." She pulled the paper back and saw the gerbera daisies. "Well, Guy, it was really sweet of you and all, but I am really not the daisy type."

"Hey, hey, don't touch." Guy grabbed the daisies from her and tossed them on the back seat. "Those are for her. This is for you." And from his inside suit pocket he pulled a blue Tiffany's box and dropped it on her lap. "Now let's get going, I'm starving." He turned and winked at Diana. "In more ways than one."

Diana grimaced at his attempt to be lecherous, but pulled the car door shut. While they drove to her apartment, Diana opened the Tiffany box. Inside was a large Elsa Peretti floating heart pendant in gold. Predictable. Still, it would make a nice Christmas present for her mom.

"You like?" Guy asked, glancing over at her, eager for her reaction.

"Guy, you are so thoughtful." She leaned over and gave him a soft kiss on the neck, running her tongue along it the way she knew he liked. "Now let's get home and fuck."

Back at home, Miranda changed Isabella and took her out into the garden. She laid a blanket out on the lawn and put Isabella down on it in the shade of the tree. Isabella promptly fell asleep, her little chest rising and falling in steady rhythm. Kitty Cat came and sat on the corner of the blanket.

As if she were guarding Isabella, Miranda thought.

Kitty Cat watched Miranda weed the flowerbed and when Miranda looked up at her, Kitty Cat squinted her eyes shut in a cat's kiss. Miranda dug deep in the dirt, rooting out weeds. Between her fingers worms struggled to get back underground when she had exposed them, little beetles with triangular red backs strutted away from her, and each tenacious, white, hairy weed root gave a silent scream when she ripped it from the earth. It was good for Miranda to be close to the earth at this time, to participate in a small way in the necessary killing that made it possible for other things to grow.

I'll call Evelyn when I'm done, she thought, ripping another strangling weed from the ground. She tossed it on the pile with the rest that were slowly withering in the sun, dead from the minute they were separated from their soil.

As soon as they got to Diana's apartment, Guy headed for her bathroom. Using the toothbrush he kept there, he brushed his teeth vigorously. Diana came up behind him.

"Did you have onions or something for lunch?"

Guy shook his head and spit into the sink. "No, a fucking hair in my teeth. One of Miranda's. She's a goddamn hairy beast. It's been driving me nuts all day."

Diana watched him. Guy rinsed his mouth out using the tumbler by the sink. For a moment they stood there and stared at each other in the mirror.

"Poor prince," Diana said. "Climbing up Rapunzel's hair expecting to find a princess and instead you find a witch." ·

Guy turned around and pulled Diana to him. He kissed her hard, twining his hands in her short curls. "Don't let's talk about it anymore," he mumbled into her neck, pushing her toward the bedroom with his body.

Miranda gave Isabella her dinner and bath. In the tub she carefully soaped Isabella's round pink limbs and rinsed her with a plastic cup. Isabella crowed and splashed the water with hands that looked like starfish, her duck-curl slick against her scalp. Kitty Cat watched from the bathroom doorway for a few moments, but when the droplets of water started flying, she made a leisurely exit to the kitchen where she curled up on a chair. Miranda towelled and powdered Isabella, kissing her again and again on her sweet neck and soft cheek. She put her down in her crib and turned on the mobile. Pretty, good fairies with glittering wings danced around and around. Isabella watched, entranced. Miranda closed the door softly and went to the kitchen.

In the bright kitchen, all gleaming surfaces and stainless steel appliances, Miranda pulled the recipe from between the pages of an *O* magazine. The paper on which the recipe was written was much creased, almost transparent from handling with oily hands. The edges were torn and there were hardened blotches and splotches. The writing was faint, but Miranda could still read it. In fact it was such a simple recipe she almost knew it by heart and only pulled out the paper to check her own memory against it.

Kitty Cat watched Miranda as she stirred and patted and filled the piecrust. She yawned when the clock struck ten, her pink cat mouth opening so wide it almost obscured the rest of her face. She sniffed at the pie as Miranda carefully pulled three hairs from her own head and laid them across the centre.

Miranda batted Kitty Cat on the nose, saying, "That's not for you." Kitty Cat knew it wasn't for her, so she fixed Miranda with a cold eye and then began to lick her paw.

When Miranda brought the cherry pie, Guy's favourite, out of the oven, Kitty Cat twined round and round her ankles, purring and rubbing her cheek against Miranda's leg. She carefully set the pie in the middle of the kitchen table.

Miranda turned off the downstairs lights and went up. She ran a hot bath and decided to wash her hair in the tub, something she rarely did because it meant having to stand up under the shower and rinse it off after the bath was finished. It wasn't like in those romantic movies where the husband lovingly lathered and sluiced water over his wife's hair as she sat in an old-fashioned claw foot tub, his soapy administrations inevitably leading to sex. Still, she loved the way it felt to work lather through her hair, all the way to the ends, each strand winding around her fingers and when she pulled them out, the hair would stretch across them for a moment: a web of hair with glistening bubbles of soap caught in it like opalescent fish eyes that would burst when she tugged her fingers all the way through. She thought of her conversation with Evelyn that afternoon.

"Miranda,"—Evelyn's voice had sounded high, hysterical—"the pathologist couldn't believe it when they opened him up." Here Evelyn had broken into a fit *of giggles. "He said it was as if his heart was clogged like a drain with hair in it. Strands of something were wound around his aorta; the inside of his heart was full of it. Like those terrible pictures you see at the vet of heartworms inside dogs' hearts."*

Miranda stood up and rinsed her hair out, letting it cover her face and the water run off it in sheets as if she had no face, as if she was nothing more than a silky ripple of tresses, the indicator of fertility.

Guy was dressing in the half-light from the bathroom. Diana sat up in bed and watched him, sheets pulled up to her bare breasts. She noted ungenerously the thickening around his torso, the slight droop of his buttocks, the thinning patch at the back of his head.

"If I were your wife, I'd kill you."

"That's why you're not."

Guy leaned over and kissed her goodbye, trailing his hand across the top of her breasts.

He whistled as he got into his SUV, the comfortable leather seats surrounding him like plump arms, the blinking lights of the dashboard the eyes of an indulgent mother winking at his indiscretion, twinkling with approval that her boy was a man, a real man. He steered out onto the street with one hand on the steering wheel, one arm resting on the window ledge. He thought about Miranda, tucked up in bed in one of her white nighties, mouth fallen open, the little purr she made when she was deeply asleep. He thought about the flowers he had bought for Miranda. He probably should have taken them in and put them in water, but he hadn't thought he would be at Diana's so late. It was already eleven. Their colours would be faded, the leaves beginning to curl under.

Oh well, it's the thought that counts. He was very pleased with himself.

After her shower, Miranda tiptoed in to check on Isabella. In the dim glow from the clown nightlight the room seem suspended in an enchantment: the motionless pink rocker with its gingham ruffle, the white wicker dresser and the twining roses on the rug. The stuffed animals ranged round the walls seemed to be frozen in anticipation of her leaving, when they would resume their nocturnal roamings and rustlings. Only their eyes gleamed, the low light on the glass making it look as if they were blinking. The shadow across the stuffed dog's mouth pulled his lip back into a snarl. Looking into the crib, Miranda saw Kitty Cat. The cat put back her ears and hissed at her.

Suck the breath out of babies, they suck the breath ... But Isabella was fine. Her eyes were open and she was watching her mother.

Miranda lifted a spitting Kitty Cat out of the crib. "Go out, Kitty." But the cat ran under the rocker where she hunched down. Miranda picked Isabella up and swayed with her to and fro, in the ancient rhythms that ran through every mother, the rhythm of the water that humans came from. She would keep her daughter safe from harm, the poor little fatherless girl, she would keep her safe.

The hair was back. Guy could feel it again. The damn thing was tickling his throat. It felt as if it were growing down his throat, touching and twining as it slid down. Guy yanked the rear view mirror over to see if he could pull it out. He stuck a hand in his mouth and tugged, but the hair wound round and down, he could feel it grazing his tonsils, as if a small fly was caught in his throat, its wings vibrating with maddening accuracy. He had to get it out—it was choking him. Guy gagged and tried to cough it up but still it filled his throat and finally he took his hands off the wheel and frantically scraped at his mouth but it wouldn't come, and the car spun out of control and crashed into the cement barrier.

Miranda tucked Isabella back in her crib. This was Isabella's kingdom and the animals kept watch, because even roses had thorns. And Miranda slept alone in her blood-red nightgown, the cool and empty bed her reward.

The Family

The family's house was a rambling white-frame farmhouse set on a hill. It had attics and dormers and porches. To her it seemed like there were twenty, forty, even fifty children in the family, but the actual count was thirteen. Like a family of rabbits in a warren on the hill, instead of underneath it. Not all the children lived at home; a few were off at university or had jobs in the city, but there were still enough to make the house feel perpetually in chaos.

Adelaide was a distant cousin, spending the summer with the family ostensibly as a sort of babysitter, but the parents were never far from home. The children's parents, Ruth and Jim, spent a good deal of their time in the outbuildings that served as their business, where they spun and dyed the wool from their own sheep, and then knit it into fabulous and bizarre sweaters, hats, scarves. Their company, Au Natural, was known for its striking colour combinations and the way they had of constructing the knit pieces so that they seemed to float, or to hang just ready to fall apart. They'd even had designers from Europe and fashion editors at the farm to see the pieces and order things for collections. These fashionable people always left delighted with the modesty of Ruth and Jim, who ran Au Natural like they ran their family, with a charming negligence and trust in the ability of everyone to pull their own weight. They were known as good neighbours, unpretentious successes, and the best of the new-era hippies who combined style with eco-awareness.

Adelaide had to admit that the children, despite their absolute lack of respect for her or any other authority figure except their parents, kept themselves constructively busy. They built tree forts, put together little books with their own drawings and collages, knitted doll clothes under the trees in the orchard, rode their horses wildly, but not recklessly, and cared for their rabbits, ducks, dogs and cats without being reminded to. They were polite to Adelaide, but sometimes cut their eyes away when she was talking to them, to indulge in a secret amusement amongst themselves. Sometimes they would stare with wide-open eyes at her, as if she were speaking a foreign language when she tried to direct them to sit down at the table for lunch, or some such thing.

Then one of them would shout, "A picnic!" And before she could say anything they would grab blankets and pillows, the older children filling a large willow basket with leftovers and bottles of lemonade. A picnic would be spread beside the brook that meandered behind the house, under a tree, the children eating, talking about books they had read or the antics of their pets, while Adelaide sat helpless, a way off on a large pillow thoughtfully set by them in the shade of the tree, and watched. Often their parents would stumble on these idyllic scenes and smile and the children would surround them vying for attention, and Ruth or Jim would tell Adelaide she was doing a really terrific job, they were so happy she had joined them that summer and the children would look at her with their secretive eyes to see what she would say.

If she began to say, "Oh, it wasn't . . ." they would roar and start some sort of noisy sport, or begin to tickle her until everyone was laughing, but Adelaide could feel their hard fingers scratching at her under the guise of play and she wished that the summer was over.

One of the children in particular regarded Adelaide with absolute disdain. Her name was Mary Matilda, and she was sometimes called Mattie, and sometimes Mary Mat, or just M. Adelaide, in her own fit of rebelliousness, called her nothing but Mary Matilda. The little girl was about nine or ten, with a dark fringe of hair over her forehead and her mother's blue eyes in a face still round with baby fat. But her skin, a matte white under the dark hair and the eyebrows like a raven's feather promised beauty later on. She never spoke to Adelaide unless pressed and always refused to do whatever Adelaide said— not with any anger, but with the calm assurance of authority. She would turn on her heel and go out to the stables or the yard, leaving Adelaide speechless. Adelaide didn't dare grab hold of her arm or shoulder and call her back, because Mary Matilda was a great favourite among her siblings and they watched after one another with unusual devotion.

All the children were good riders, but Mary Matilda was the best of all. That summer she generally rode bareback. Adelaide would stand by the house while the children raced down the long winding drive overhung with trees on their horses. One of the boys, Edward, would lie along one of the long tree limbs and wave a flag for them to start. The children would gallop down the drive, coming to such an abrupt stop at the end that their horses' hindquarters, foamed with sweat, would seem to almost crumple under the effort.

Mary Matilda almost always won. The only one who could beat her was her older brother Matthew.

Adelaide complained to Ruth and Jim, worried that the children would get hurt.

Ruth laughed and said, "The children have been riding since they were born."

"Before, honey, before they were born. You were riding horses into your third trimester." Jim laid his arm along his wife's shoulders. "Just about gave old Doc Johnston a heart attack." He looked at Adelaide and winked. "Don't worry, Adelaide, we won't hold you responsible if anyone breaks their neck on your watch." Then he leaned over and kissed Ruth in a way that made Adelaide blush.

Matthew, at sixteen, was the oldest of the boys still at home. His eyes were reddish brown and quite large. He used them a lot when begging favours for himself: to go down to the creek at night, to sleep on the porch when it got too hot in his attic bedroom, favours that Adelaide knew he only asked her permission for as a courtesy. He would have done what he wanted anyway. Matthew would throw his long legs and arms into various attitudes of supplication as he lay down beside Adelaide on the grass and asked her what she was reading, or if she wanted lemonade. He grinned at her with white teeth, his eyes peering from beneath a flop of sandy curls. He asked Adelaide about her friends and the city where she went to school, propped his chin in his long-fingered hands while he listened, his oddly delicate wrist bones sticking well out from his too-small jersey sleeves.

Matthew was considerate of the younger children and played their games, let them sit on his knee while he read to them. On rainy days, Mary Matilda and the others would fall in a heap on him while he sat on the old sofa in front of the fireplace in the living room and told stories.

Often while he was playing hide and seek with the children or croquet, he would leave the game and come and sit beside Adelaide to talk. Once he showed her a poem he had written; another time, he put an arm around her when they looked at a book Adelaide had brought from home. When she shrugged out from underneath, he had looked at her with the same wide eyes all the children had, guileless.

Adelaide did nothing to encourage his puppy crush, but admitted to herself she found it comforting amidst the general disregard the others treated her with.

The only house rule was that two hours in the afternoon, at the height of the day, was to be quiet time. The children were expected to go to their bedrooms and read, or sleep. None of the children ever disobeyed this rule and Adelaide was always surprised at how quietly and quickly they went up to their rooms and shut the doors. The house would fall silent, except for the sonorous ticking of the grandfather clock that stood in the entryway. Adelaide usually went out to the kitchen porch and sat on the porch swing, where she read or looked out over the well-tended gardens and land of the family's farm. Sometimes Matthew would join her, bringing a drink or a book, and they would talk softly until the first of the children came down. He didn't come all the time, not too often, because he said his parents would be disappointed if he did not set a good example for the younger children by keeping the one house rule.

When he did come, Adelaide found herself having fun for the first time that summer while she watched him goof around for her, imitating visitors to the farm, or when she caught him staring at her with his wide brown eyes, eager for her approval.

One night near the end of the summer, as the family sat at the long trestle table having dinner in the farmhouse kitchen, Ruth and Jim announced they had some news to share with them. The children, polite, attentive, listened while their parents told them that Marcus and Jane, their oldest siblings, would be coming home tomorrow. Secondly, Au Natural had just signed a contract with Devaughn, the British rock star, to provide dyed wools for the line of eco-correct clothing he and his wife had started, called Gardun, which would mean a trip to London for the whole family. Lastly, Ruth and Jim had decided to adopt a baby from Africa, a little girl whose father was dead from AIDS and whose mother could not afford to keep her any longer.

The children broke out in their own carefully controlled uproar, which always struck Adelaide as being somehow scripted.

"A baby? Can I name her?"

"I can't wait to see Marcus and show him the new pony."

"Is Jane bringing her boyfriend?"

"Are we going to be rich, Mummy?"

"Do you think we can go backstage to Devaughn's show?"

Jim and Ruth laughed and answered questions animatedly, the fingers flying as they described various things, their arms flung out in gestures, with much theatrical hugging of the children closest to them.

Matthew winked at Adelaide, and she noticed that only Mary Matilda sat silent.

The next day during the quiet hours, Adelaide sat on the porch and waited for Matthew. She assumed his wink meant he wanted to talk to her about his parents' news, that they shared a secret amusement at the whole thing. As she looked out over the garden and watched the small figure of Jim or Ruth, hard to tell from this distance, walk from shed to barn, she heard a step behind her. Adelaide turned and smiled, but it was Mary Matilda.

"Mary Matilda, it's quiet time." Adelaide felt a little tremor go through her—what if Matthew came down now and Mary Matilda saw and started a general mutiny? Matthew would never come down again during quiet time.

"I'm not sleepy." Adelaide's worry deepened. For that matter, what if Ruth or Jim came and saw Mary Matilda on the porch instead of in her room? They would know she had failed, that she had no authority over their so-well-behaved children.

"Mary Matilda, you don't have to sleep. Just lie there and read. You know the rules." Adelaide stood up.

Mary Matilda looked at her. "My necklace is caught in my hair and it pulls. Can you come upstairs and fix it?"

"I can fix it here, turn around."

"No, upstairs." Mary Matilda went in the house and Adelaide followed, knowing Mary Matilda was quite capable of causing uproar if it would make Adelaide look bad. She knew in that moment that the child in front of her, with the straight dark hair almost to her waist, the firm legs of an outdoor girl burnished with tan, the childish shoulder blades that fluttered under her striped t-shirt, hated Adelaide. Adelaide knew she hated this little girl right back, that she wanted to slap her for her insolence. There was no corporal punishment allowed of course, but Adelaide felt that Mary Matilda and her attitude would only benefit from a few well-placed spankings.

When they came to Mary Matilda's small room, a little cubby hole really, with roses on the wallpaper and a small bed with a chenille coverlet, an overflowing bookcase and dresser, a closet door ajar, she lost her temper.

"Mary Matilda, lie down right now."

"My hair, it's caught. It pulls. It hurts."

Adelaide wheeled Mary Matilda around quickly, lifted her hair and saw that, just as she thought, the child wasn't wearing a necklace.

"Get in that bed, or I'll tell your parents."

Mary Matilda's face closed like a flower shutting for the night and she lay down rigid on her bed. Adelaide left the room and pulled the door almost shut behind her, not closing it so she could see if Mary Matilda was going to stay in her room. Adelaide would look for Matthew and tell him what happened so that if Mary Matilda made any more trouble, maybe he could stop it. She could see the little girl motionless on the bed, her white arm rigid at her side, and after a heartbeat, Adelaide began to walk down the hall.

Then she heard whispers.

Walking back silently to Mary Matilda's door, wondering what trick the brat was playing on her now, she stopped just outside it and listened.

"Don't worry, the bitch went back downstairs. Come on M, if you're good, I'll let you win the next race." The voice was Matthew's.

Through the crack she saw his long limbs climbing on the narrow bed, the long-fingered hands tugging at something.

Standing in the hall frozen, her hand at her mouth, now she heard whispers all around her, heard the soft noises, like animals in their secret places, where there wasn't any light.

Meadowdene Estates

Their friends had moved into one of the new houses, at the very edge of the development outside of the city.

"It backs onto meadow still," Lorna told her over the phone. "You'd almost think we were in the country, except all those back parcels have already been sold. I'm glad. It gives me the creeps to see that empty meadow behind us, no stores, no streets. The neighbour kids like it though, always off back there with dirt bikes and wagons."

"I guess that's how it got its name," Sarah said, idly drawing a little house on the pad beside the phone.

"How what got its name?"

"Your development, Meadowdene Estates. I always wondered how they named those things. They always plough under or build over the creeks or pines, or flatten the hills so you can't tell what it looked like originally. So you don't know if it ever actually was a meadow or whatever." Sarah added a little curl of smoke to the house's chimney.

"I guess so. Look I've got to go, but you and Bill

come on Saturday and we'll have dinner on the deck. Bring a bottle of wine. I'll send directions. Maybe Jake and I can even convince you guys to buy out here."

Sarah hung up the phone and looked at her little house. She added a tree that towered over it and some bushes along the front. She thought about Lorna gloating over her new house. *Master en suite*, she'd said, sounding like she was rolling a candy around on her tongue, *eat-in kitchen*, *walk-in closets*.

Sarah crumpled her drawing and tossed it into the garbage can in the corner of the tiny kitchen. Those houses were cheap, a mortgage payment almost the same as what they paid in rent on this one-bedroom apartment downtown.

"Meadowdene Estates," Sarah said to the empty kitchen, tasting the words in her mouth.

"All these houses look alike," Bill said, turning the car down the street named Paradise Glenway, "those ugly double garages covering the front. Who the hell can tell one from the other, you can't even see the numbers."

"Like mouths," Sarah said, craning her head out the window to see if she could find the street sign for Lorna's street.

"What?"

"The garages look like mouths. Lorna's street

should be coming up soon. Utopia Gateway. It's one of the very last streets."

"Thank Jesus. Let's not linger too long, I hate this suburban shit." Bill jerked the car down the next street. Identical house after identical house flowed past them. People had tried to give their homes some personality with wreaths of plastic flowers on the half-hidden front doors, and plaster geese or rabbits on the steps, but the beige consistency of the houses defeated all attempts at decoration and made them look cheap and flimsy.

Children played in the drives, while their parents watered tiny beds of flowers beside the garages. Older kids on bikes rode past, hunched over the handlebars.

How do they know which home to go to when it's dark? Sarah wondered. *How can they tell the difference if they go too far away?*

All over the development there was the smell of barbecues going, and the hiss of unseen sprinklers. Maybe there was something more behind the solid façade of house. Sarah imagined a lawn with chairs set out or a space to play badminton or croquet. A picnic table set for early dinner. She knew there were no trees, no mature trees. They'd only seen little spindly ones with white tape-wrapped trunks and wires to hold them up on some of the mini front lawns. But maybe there'd be flowering bushes at least in the yards, lilac or peony, something scented and old-fashioned.

They found Lorna and Jake's house after two more wrong turns. They pulled into the wide spotless driveway. Bill closed his eyes. "Dinner and out, right? I honestly don't want to try to find my way out of this hellhole in the dark."

Sarah didn't answer. She was staring at the empty lot beside Lorna's house. Tall grass waved in it, and there was the low hum of crickets or grasshoppers coming from its green depths. On the other side of the lot was another house. Then the street ended, and the gilded meadow reasserted itself, spikes of grass as high as Sarah's head beckoned in the sun as they moved with the breeze.

"She didn't say there was an empty lot next to her." A rap on her window startled Sarah. A distorted face smiled at her from the other side of the safety glass. Sarah opened the door and stepped out into the drive, a little unsteady from the long drive. A nylon flag that said *Friends Welcome*, with an appliqué pineapple beneath it, floated over the open doorway to the house.

"Hey, stranger." Lorna gave Sarah a hug. "You guys made it. Come on in."

Bill and Jake were already heading toward the house. Lorna walked ahead of Sarah, who followed, the paper bag with wine in it forgotten in the back seat.

Lorna and Jake took them on a tour of the house. A finished basement: "This is where I'm gonna keep my tools, man, and my beer fridge," Jake told them with a wink to Bill.

"A Jacuzzi tub, can you believe it?" Lorna showed them the beige marble-look bathroom. "I soak in here for hours."

"Yeah, sometimes I think I married a fish. But you know what they say about women—"

"Jake, that's nasty!" Lorna laughed and punched his arm. "You folks must be hungry. Jake fired up the barbecue a while ago. Sarah and I can make the salad while you guys put the steaks on."

Lorna and Sarah stood in the bright, big kitchen, tearing lettuce and chopping carrots and talking about people they had known when they worked together as legal secretaries at the same downtown firm.

"God, remember him? He was such an asshole." Lorna took a sip from the glass of wine she had poured when they came downstairs. She had been laughing and her face was flushed. Sarah remembered that liquor hit Lorna hard. She watched Lorna's hands tear the lettuce with coarse motions and toss it into the big glass bowl. Lorna moved between fridge and chopping block, in easy ownership of the oversized kitchen. The silence that fell between them seemed to reflect in the polished surfaces of the appliances. In the city, it had been simple just being couples together, meeting at noisy restaurants or in close-packed bars. You could talk easily for an hour or two about who was moving, who bought a house, how crazy the prices in the city were, parking problems, space problems . . . then you went home and felt you'd had a good night out with friends.

Sarah swirled the wine in the bloated, pink-tinted glass Lorna had given her earlier, but didn't drink. "What's the deal with that lot next to you?"

"Interested?" Lorna shook the salad dressing and poured it into the bowl. "Well, someone owns it, but they're waiting to build on it. Something to do with a bad foundation, water, or sand, or something. They're gonna bring in bulldozers and dig it up pretty soon, I guess."

They carried the salad out through the sliding glass doors onto the deck.

"Welcome to our little piece of paradise." Jake raised a beer in Sarah's direction and threw his other arm wide.

He and Bill were standing next to an expensive gas barbecue on which meat cooked; the blood red of the flesh crisped and blackened in the flame. The deck they were on filled the back yard, but there was a small strip of dirt between the fence and the deck's edge in which some anaemic-looking impatiens drooped. Steps led off the deck on one side to a cement path that curved around to the front of the house. If you stood at the edge of the deck and stretched, you could almost touch the chain-link fence that separated their deck from the neighbours'. Sarah had known the houses were close together, but she had thought that at least in the back they had scaled them down, so there was room for them to breathe at least.

She realized this idea of breathing was ridiculous, that you wanted the most house for your money. Why else buy a house if not to have lots of space inside, to put things, to live? Behind the back fence, the meadow grasses waved, sank and rose again under the constant eddies of air.

They sat at the table on the deck, shaded by a green market umbrella that Lorna proudly announced she had bought on sale at Wal-Mart. The other three ate their steak and salad, forks travelling to their mouths with a mechanical rapidity. They exclaimed over the thickness, the size of the cuts. Sarah cut into her own steak, but when the red juice squirted onto her plate, she put her fork down. Even the salad sitting in its oily dressing was unappetizing. The bubbles of oil looked to her like little mouths popping open among the glossy green leaves.

"God, that's good," Bill said, taking a swig of his

beer. "I could get used to this, barbecuing on the deck, Jacuzzi tub waiting upstairs."

"I told Sarah you guys should think about moving out here. We love it. We don't miss the dirt and noise of the city at all." Lorna poured herself another glass of wine. Sarah noticed the bottle was almost empty and she was still nursing her first glass.

"Who owns that house on the other side of the lot?" Sarah asked.

"Now that is the $64,000 dollar question, my dear." Jake burped and took another swig of his beer. "Or should I say $264,000 dollar question?"

Bill laughed and clinked his beer bottle against Jake's. In the city he had always referred to Jake as a crude bastard. He had never wanted to go out with them as couples. Only after much pleading on Sarah's part had he condescended to spend this evening together. Now she couldn't catch his eye to suggest they leave. Bill leaned back in his chair, his attention on the new bottle of beer in his hands, head tilted to catch another of Jake's stupid jokes.

Lorna leaned in to Sarah in boozy confidentiality. Sarah could smell the meat and alcohol on her breath, and recoiled just a little. Lorna didn't notice.

"That house," Lorna said, leaning even closer, "belonged to this young couple. Newlyweds, I guess. Moved in, furnished it and then, boom—" Lorna clapped her hands together and sat back in her chair. "Gone. No one knows what the story is. There haven't been any police, or moving vans. No relatives. If you look at the house closely, it looks like someone tried to pull the front door right off its hinges, but all the furniture's still just sitting there." Lorna leaned forward and pointed at Sarah. "Me, I'm not that nosey, that's just what one of the neighbours told me. No one goes near it. Not even the kids. Let me tell you, it's weird as hell. I guess they're gonna come and do something about it soon, at least that's what someone told me. I mean, they're developing all that goddamn grass back there soon, so they *have* to do something about the place." She looked into her empty glass. "Hey, Sarah didn't you say you were bringing some wine?"

"I forgot to bring it in. It's in the car."

Lorna looked at her, her eyes unfocussed and narrow.

"Why don't you go get it, babe?" Bill asked. He smiled at her from behind his beer bottle.

Sarah got up and went down the steps to the walkway next to Lorna's house. On the other side of her, the house next door was so close she could run her hand over its siding as she walked. From behind her, she heard a burst of laughter, Lorna's voice rising above it for a moment, then sinking back into the slurred hilarity. The two houses blocked the sun and the pathway was cold. Sarah was glad when she made it to the open driveway and saw the empty lot with the grasses bowing in the sun. For a minute she seriously thought about getting into the car and leaving Bill here, but it really wouldn't be worth the fight that would follow.

She opened the back door of the car and grabbed the bottle of wine out of its paper bag. She had bought it the day before at the LCBO in the middle of the busy city, three blocks from her apartment, across from the park where squirrels scrambled up full-grown trees and old men sat on park benches feeding the pigeons, and the concrete overpass had *Tori loves Amy* spray-painted in bright red balloon letters.

Utopia Gateway was deserted, the street quiet except for faint noises coming from behind the big blank houses, the clean mouths of the garages closed tight.

Sarah stepped into the street and walked past the empty lot. The buzz of the grasshoppers grew louder and one of them jumped on her foot, then spread its black-and-white marked wings and flew back into the grass. A child's bike lay half hidden in the long weeds, shiny, the plastic flowers on its basket bright. On the other side of the lot was the empty house, its garage shut as tightly as the others on the street. It looked exactly like Lorna and Jake's house. Sarah walked up the short cement path to the front door.

There was no nylon flag hanging here. The front door was ajar, hanging half off hinges that were pulled out of the frame almost completely. Sarah stood there for a moment. From the doorway came a cool and patient silence. The bottle of wine slipped from her hand and shattered on the cement steps, pooling red down them. One, then two yellow jackets appeared and began to suck at the spilled wine, their lower segments going up and down in furious intent as they worked. Sarah twisted past the broken door and entered the front hall.

The house was completely furnished. The dining room to the left of the front door had a table set for dinner with gold-rimmed china and wine glasses. Sarah counted four places. A bottle of wine with dust on its shoulders stood on a nearby sideboard. In the curio cabinet near the doorway were crystal vases, and wedding photographs of a young couple in silver frames. Sarah didn't walk into the room. She stood in the doorway, and looked, not wanting to disturb anything. On the other side of the front hall was the living room. Sarah remembered this layout from Lorna and Jake's house. The door to this room was partly shut. Again, the wood in the frame showed raw, as if someone had tried to pull the door off its hinges. Through the gap Sarah could see a sofa, a magazine lying on a coffee table, a stereo and television in an entertainment unit.

She stepped back from the ruined door and stood in the centre of the hall, perfectly still, her breath as shallow as she could make it. On a small table under a mirror in the hall was a ceramic bowl with keys and change in it. The late afternoon sun coming through the windows on either side of the door lit the keys into gold. Her reflection in the mirror was almost obliterated by the intensity of the dying light. She held her breath and felt the house breathe in and out, waiting.

Upstairs a door opened. Sarah moved to the foot of the staircase. She couldn't see the top of the stairs in the light pouring down from the window on the landing. Overhead another door shut. She touched the banister with her hand. Behind her there was a soft whisper, the sound of wind through uncut grass.

Sarah began to ascend the stairs. With each step upward she dissolved further into a stylized silhouette against the pitiless light.

Salvage

She finished folding his shirts from the wardrobe and laid them neatly on top of the pants in the crate. Since coming on board the ship she had finished cleaning out half of the crew's cabins; tomorrow she would finish the other five. Then the salvage crew would load the stuff on board their shuttle and make the two-week trip back to the station.

She began to work on the chest of drawers next to the bunk. It was always almost unbearably intimate to be folding and packing away a stranger's things. Their clothing, photos, mementos, even mundane objects like their coffee mugs, often left with a slosh of liquid still in them or a crescent of lipstick on the rim, she washed them out, folded them, covered them in bubble wrap and packed them in the crates, as if the person were having them sent to a new address. Instead, the crates would be sent to next of kin. If there were no living relatives, or the family didn't want the crates, the usable items would be sent to charity, personal photos and papers burned. Nothing was wasted on any of the company's ships.

In the bottom of the top drawer of the dresser,

she found a journal. A small red book, with the crewmember's name on the cover. They weren't supposed to read the papers of the people they salvaged, but sometimes she would look, would read the half-finished letter, or the inscription on the back of a photograph. She opened the book to the first page. Her headset squawked.

"We're about ready to go to half-light. Are you going to bed down there for the night?"

"Yeah, I'll finish this one up first thing in the morning."

"We'll call you for breakfast."

"Thanks. Good night."

The lights in the cabin dimmed. She stripped the sheets and pillows from the bed and placed them into a plastic bag. Then she unrolled her own sleeping bag and spread it on the bunk. She undressed and slid into it. The button above her head would turn off the lights, but she reached for the journal instead.

This crewmember had been youngish, married, with a daughter. He had been part of the computer section of the ship. She was interested in people, their flesh, their faces, and their minds. That's why she had asked to work in personal effects salvage. The others on the salvage team would rip out computers and furniture; later another team would come for the metal and wire, only she packed away clothes and pictures like a relative, like a lover.

She knew nothing about the technology of these ships and didn't care. Why they ran, or why they sometimes didn't. This ship looked fine to her, but it was useless, would no longer travel, and could only float through space suspended by something she knew nothing about. She imagined she knew about as much about it as the average person had known a thousand years ago about air travel. If you lived with it, you took it for granted.

The station had received the distress signal, but by the time the emergency staff had reached the ship, the crew was gone. Food had been left on tables, computers running, even a satellite broadcast movie playing on the screen in the recreation room. It was assumed the crew had taken off in the shuttle for some reason and the shuttle had been destroyed in flight. But no detritus was found and no clues were left on the computers.

So this ship floated here like some modern-day *Marie Celeste*, giving up nothing of its story.

She opened the journal at random. Despite all the predictions, they had never eradicated paper or writing with a pen completely. There was still something in the visceral act of writing, the dance between the brain and the hand that was satisfying. He had spiky handwriting that was a bit uneven. Like most men, his writing looked younger than he had been.

The entry that she opened read:

It is late at night and the ship is asleep. This is the time when it is hell for insomniacs, when everyone else is off in a dream, and you are alone in the night. The objects in the room take on sinister meaning. The photograph seems to watch you, its face contorted, the chair to move closer, the clock to keep track of every heartbeat.

She flipped to another page:

If I think of the reality of the ship suspended, the endless sky above and below, black and unfathomable and me in the centre of this fallible construct I begin to understand what death must be like. The fear of non-existence, a concept ungraspable in its implications, its depths of unending nothing. It is truly the only reality.

She turned to the last page. It said:

With everything we know, we know nothing.

She shut the journal and put it on the floor next to the bunk. The lights flickered, a glitch on the dying ship, and she reached up and pushed the button to turn them off. The cabin was black and she was alone.

His fears didn't touch her, she was there to salvage

him, she still existed. Her heart beat *I am I am* as she lay on her side. She began to drift off to sleep.

There was a hollow pounding at the door to the cabin. It stopped, then began again.

"Coming, coming."

She sat up and pushed the lights on, but they didn't respond. She got out of the bunk and felt her way past the dresser to the door. The pounding hadn't stopped.

She stood just behind the door and called, "Who is it? For Chrissakes, what's going on?"

The noise stopped and she reached out and pulled the door open.

The long hallway was empty and dark, lit only by red safety lights along the bottom of the walls. It was night and she was the only one awake.

The next morning the sunrise simulation lights in the cabins came up and she lay for a while in the sleeping bag on the bunk, getting her bearings. The soft padding of the bunk's ceiling and sides was supposed to be soothing, but the image that came to her mind was a padded cell and her trussed in the sleeping bag as if it were a straightjacket. She wondered what going mad was like. Did you feel the slide into madness? Was it a relief to finally let go of the constraints of reality and just act on the impulses you formerly had to fight?

The intercom above her head squawked, "Are you coming down for breakfast, Richards? Or are you waiting for room service?"

She hit the button to reply. "Jesus, I'll be right down, Thompson, hold your fucking impatient horses."

"Language, language, Richards." There was a deep laugh and muffled conversation, then the connection cut out.

She gave the intercom the finger, and took a quick shower. They wouldn't have water for much longer. The salvage team figured just enough for the three days it would take them to clear the ship. As she dressed, she thought about the banging on the door last night; she'd confront those assholes at breakfast. Just because she was the only woman on this team didn't mean she was going to put up with a bunch of practical jokes meant to remind her she didn't have a turkey neck and coconuts hanging between her legs. She'd known that for a long time and was grateful.

The ten-man salvage team was in the mess. From the smells, she could tell it was eggs, various breakfast meats and strong coffee on the menu today. She slipped in next to Sahid, the crew's medic and grabbed a plate and fork from the centre of the table. Then she helped herself to the steaming dishes on the table's built-in hotplates. Sahid, who was one of the good guys, passed her a mug of coffee. She took a few swallows and allowed the caffeine to blow away the last of the cobwebs. She set down her mug.

"Okay, you fuckers, who was playing practical jokes last night?"

Thompson looked up from his plate. He was redheaded, with muscle-bound arms and a chest that was wider than she was, and in charge of the equipment salvage, which meant the rest of the team. Although she was really at the same corporate level as he was and was the only one in charge of personal effects salvage, Thompson didn't see it that way. Thompson's success with minor admin assistants on the base had convinced him that he was God and he expected every woman to play the part of recent convert.

"Well, Richards, just what do you mean?" He crossed his arms, so that it looked like two baby piglets being hugged to his bulging chest.

"That banging on my door last night. Which one of you morons was it?" She addressed the table at large but locked eyes with Thompson, assuming that any joke had been undertaken with his careful direction.

"Oh, Richards, maybe it was a late night booty

call, or maybe you needing one had your mind playing tricks."

Next to her, she saw Sahid's pale brown face darken across the cheeks as he blushed. She turned to look at him swiftly, but he was looking at his plate. She pointed her knife at Thompson.

"Look, Thompson, I'd better sleep like a baby tonight, or you're going to have to answer for it."

Thompson leaned across the table and grabbed her wrist. "Answer to who, you?"

She twisted her wrist out of his hand and put the knife down beside her plate. "No, the sexual harassment committee, asshole." She picked up a link sausage and bit it neatly in two.

The first cabin she started on that morning was a woman's. It was on the port side of the ship. The woman had had a virtual window.

It had been determined in the earliest stages of long-term space travel and occupation that windows that showed the vast expanse of space—its blackness, its ability to shrink to insignificance any human action or emotion—caused episodes of deep depression, which could incapacitate a wide number of crewmembers or travellers at any time. No amount of medication or pre-screening seemed to work. It was as if the blackness of space itself sucked the will out of those who succumbed. Now, almost all ship cabins and certainly all common rooms were equipped with virtual windows. Either scenes of life on earth could be played at random, or you could set a personal program. Because earth was their home as humans, the place where they had genetically begun even if they had been born on a moon colony or on a ship somewhere in orbit—those were the scenes that restored a sense of equilibrium to travellers. Earth was the place where what they did and what they felt had some meaning, even if it was only to a few people. In space they were all like Jonah in the whale's belly—alone, with only a guttering candle to light the vastness.

Curious as to what this crewmember had programmed on her virtual window, Richards pushed the button. The window opened up onto a scene that looked like a room in one of those old Dutch paintings of the seventeenth century. There was a black and white tiled floor and diffused light was coming in from a window—not visible, though the butter yellow and soft blue heavy curtains that hung beside it were. There was a convex mirror on the wall and a wooden table and chair underneath it. On the table sat a skull and an hourglass. The virtual window provided so realistic a view, that it was possible to see the dust motes filtering down through the light and hear the faint noise of traffic: horses, people talking, even a bell tolling.

A soft scratching sound slowly became louder as a woman with a long green skirt and white blouse came into the room, sweeping. The broom swept across the tiles rhythmically. The woman paused in her work and looked out the unseen window. She seemed quite happy. She was humming a soft tune to herself and the sun fell on her wide plain face.

There was a skittering from the corner of the room and a small dog ran out. It was an odd colour, reddish black, more red than black, as if it had been singed. The colour of the barbecued meat that hung in the windows of some Chinese restaurants. It came up to the frame of the virtual window and snuffled along the edge. Richards inadvertently took a step back from the window, but the other woman seemed unaware of the dog. She had gone back to her sweeping, slow strokes like the pendulum of a clock. The dog ran back from the edge of the frame and stopped halfway across the room. It lifted its head and turned toward Richards. It was not a dog. It had a wizened face with black eyes and it grinned at her as she stared in horror. Then it turned and ran under the woman's skirt.

Richards reached forward and turned off the window.

What the hell was that about? she wondered. She turned her back on the window, to focus on the wardrobe on the wall opposite, but the skin on her back crawled. She felt that something could slide out of that window even though she had turned it off. The oblivious woman had been no less creepy than the dog. *Stop being ridiculous, it's just the bad night getting to you.*

Richards began to work methodically, clearing the items from the wardrobe, noting them in her ledger. The routine soon dissipated any lingering fears she had. She had finished the dresser and nightstand and was just clearing the desk when there was a knock at the door.

"Come in."

The door slid open. It was Sahid.

"Am I interrupting?" He stood in the doorway, rocking back and forth on his heels. Richards figured he had probably come to apologize for whatever small part Thompson had coerced him into playing in last night's effort to scare her.

"Come on in, have a seat." Richards sat in the desk chair and gestured for Sahid to sit on the bunk.

"Richards, I am very sorry about this morning. Thompson can be a real," here Sahid paused and looked down at his hands, "prick."

"Well, it wasn't very cool of you to go along with whatever game he's up to."

Sahid looked up at Richards. "No, he is a prick,

but I did not take part. I came to tell you that I heard something last night, too."

"Knocking? They were knocking on your door too?" *That was a lot of running*, Richards thought. The other members of the salvage crew had a superstitious dread of staying in vanished crewmembers' cabins. They avoided them like the plague. The only time they would enter them for any length of time was when the crates were ready to be moved and loaded. Last night, as usual, they had stayed in the guest cabins on the other side of the ship, three floors down. So they would have had to knock on Sahid's door and then run up to hers, then back down, to avoid being seen.

"It wasn't a knocking, it was more of a scratching. When I opened my door I thought I saw a small shadow running along the hall, but I couldn't be sure." Richards thought of the dog-devil in the virtual window and shivered, but that was just stupid. That was a figment of the crewmember's weird imagination, not a real animal.

"I'd guess it was just the guys trying to take the piss out of you, Sahid, like they were doing with me."

Sahid looked at Richards. His dark eyes were steady on hers and she was the one who looked away first.

"You think maybe it was more?" he asked.

"No, no, I don't. Just nerves. Usually this job doesn't get to me, but this time with Thompson running the show and none of the other members of my team . . ." Richards petered off and glanced unwittingly at the virtual window.

"Tonight," Sahid said, "I will sleep in the cabin next to you. If it is Thompson, we will catch him and it will make a stronger case for the board of directors. If it is not Thompson, then maybe we can figure out what it is."

"Are you sure, Sahid? I know how you guys hate staying in the crew cabins. Besides, there's only one more night on board this ship, then we're back to home base."

Sahid nodded. "It's true, the cabins where the crew stayed are," he looked around the small cabin they were in, as if searching for an explanation, "full of someone else's memories. But I have always wondered what the truth is about these abandoned ships. It seems to me that stripping them and leaving them to float empty does an injustice to those who have vanished. As if the crew never existed." He looked at the crates she was packing. "Only the bits and pieces you pack away prove they were here, and then even those small remains are taken away."

Richards shifted in her seat. She had always thought of her job as the one that honoured the missing, not one that put the final touches on their disappearance. Sahid stood up. "Till tonight then." And he left the cabin.

She finished two more cabins without incident. There was the same general poignancy of the abandoned things of the crewmembers, those small items that had so much history for the individual, but would have little or no meaning for anyone else, even family members or dear friends. They might be a memento, but the very complex web of associations that each person winds around something as simple as a pen on their desk, the cough lozenges in the bedside table, the worn slippers, the routines and smallest gestures ingrained in the things of their lives, could never be replicated or fully grasped. Nothing out of the usual.

She had a quick lunch of sandwiches in the mess before working on the last two cabins. Already the ship was looking empty. The lounge was stripped of all its equipment; there were still chairs and the hot table in the mess, but that would be packed up after tomorrow's breakfast. She made herself another sandwich to have for dinner. The thought of encountering Thompson and his cronies again around the table was not something she was up for. When she got back, she'd make sure she was never on another team with that redheaded jerk-off again.

After lunch she went up to the second-to-last cabin. As she stepped in, there was a brushing against her legs, as if a small animal or breeze had just moved past her into the room. Animals were not allowed on the company's ships. They reacted even worse than humans did to space travel, finding the severing of connections with earth impossible to negotiate. They seemed to be able to tell that even though the floors and furniture in the ships were solid, they were still suspended in the nowhere that was space. The animals brought on board would refuse to move, refuse to eat, snap at their owners and finally die, twitching and panting. You couldn't trick an animal's senses, not like a human's.

The cabin door slid shut behind her and she turned and looked at the right-hand wall. In big looping script was written: *Jane, I waited for you. I'm going.* The writing was in red permanent marker. Richards stepped up to it and touched it. Of course it was dry, marker didn't take very long to dry. She thought again of Thompson, but shook her head. It was too subtle for him. Maybe this was a last message one of the crewmembers had left for another. She checked the ship's original roster on her handheld computer. There had been a Jane on board; in fact, her cabin had been the one with the strange virtual window. This cabin had belonged to a man named

Adam Davies. Had they been lovers? She wondered. Friends? Where had he been going?

She walked over to the wardrobe and began to empty it. Shirts folded carefully, pants smoothed and laid on top, a navy jacket, a brown jacket. She reached down into the bottom of the wardrobe and brought out a pair of scuffed runners, some dress shoes, a pair of loafers that looked as if they had been seldom worn. She slid each one into a plastic bag and sealed it, then placed them carefully on top of the other clothes. She thought she saw something in the back of the wardrobe and knelt down and reached in as far as she could, up to her elbow. Nothing. Must have been her imagination.

Then she felt the rough bristles and a sharp nip. She pulled her hand out. Her middle finger on her right hand was bleeding.

She fell back, just stopping herself from toppling by putting out her left hand, holding her right hand to her chest. Nothing moved in the dark back of the closet; there was no glitter of animal eyes. Moving slowly, always keeping the wardrobe in view, she stood up and picked up the chair from beside the desk. With a swift motion she rammed the chair legs first into the back of the closet, sweeping it back and forth. Empty. She slammed the doors of the wardrobe shut. Adrenaline made it feel as if her veins were coursing with a river of fire, searing her beneath her skin. She backed away from the closet still clutching her right hand and into the cabin's bathroom.

Once inside, she hit the door close button and the bathroom door slid shut with a pock, metal fitting neatly into seam. Only then did she turn around and face the sink on the other wall. Her breath was coming in ragged gasps and there was a tight pain in her chest. Anxiety attack. She leaned over the metal sink, willing her breathing to slow.

You just cut your hand on something sharp, a stray pin, a rough bolt. The fur, I felt the fur. A stray pin, a rough bolt. The fur.

When her breathing had finally stopped catching and heaving, she straightened up and opened the first aid kit on the wall next to the sink. She poured the bottle of disinfectant over her finger, hands trembling. The cap of the disinfectant rattled against the metal inside the sink when she dropped it and the sound seemed to be magnified, to go on long after the cap had stopped bouncing under the flow of the disinfectant over her finger. It was the sound of someone shaking the door, trying to get in. She dropped the whole bottle into the sink, and turned to the door, but it was still, the noise had died away.

She wrapped gauze and a bandage around her finger.

A pin, a pin, a pin.

Even as the wound disappeared under the bandages, she couldn't forget that when the blood had been washed away, she had seen the imprint of a small human tooth.

For the first time ever in her career, Richards didn't finish packing up a room. She left the bathroom as quickly as she could without running and, never turning her back to the wardrobe, slipped out the cabin door. Soon it would be night and she would be trapped again on this floating coffin, this padded cell.

In the last cabin, she packed the contents without looking at any of the personal effects too closely, just wanting to be finished, to have the last of the missing crew neatly packed away in the impersonal salvage bins. The thought of the cabin next door with things still in drawers and the message in red ink on the wall made her uneasy, as if it was waiting for the occupant to return. As she latched the lid of the last bin, there was a knock on the door of the cabin.

"Come in."

It was Sahid. He was carrying a bag of sandwiches and some bottles of juice.

"I thought you might not come down for dinner."

Richards thanked him and took the sandwich that he offered her. She had left the ones she had brought up from the mess hall earlier in the cabin next door. As it was, she wasn't sure she would be able to eat.

"The night crew will be coming on in an hour. They have everything almost finished in the rest of the ship."

"Well, I'm done here, thank God," she said. "You shouldn't sleep next door tonight, Sahid, the cabin was . . ." Here she faltered, not sure if she wanted to confide in Sahid about her experience. ". . . unsettling, a bit of a mess." She looked at the sandwich in her hand and knew she would not be able to go beyond the few bites she had taken. She threw the rest of it in a garbage receptacle. Sahid watched her.

"So I should sleep down in the guest cabins again tonight?"

"No. Sahid, I was wondering if you would stay in here with me tonight."

Sahid said nothing, just nodded. They spent the last half hour before lights-out in silence. She finished packing up the bedside table, crated the contents and then ducked into the bathroom to get ready for bed. Sahid laid his sleeping bag out on the floor of the cabin, his medic kit next to it, and after she was done in the bathroom he went in. She could hear him brushing his teeth, the water running. It seemed a very intimate sound, that of a live person in close proximity.

She had never lived with anyone except her family when she was young. There had been some lovers, some boyfriends, but no one that she had felt close enough to share the everyday motions of life with.

Now, hearing Sahid, she wondered if she had made a mistake. It was a comfort to listen to another person perform the same tasks she did on a daily basis, to feel that there was something that extended human to human, that tethered them even when they floated in the unknowable reaches of space.

Sahid slid into his sleeping bag. The headset she had set on the nightstand squawked. "We're going to half-light." It sounded like Thompson, but she couldn't be sure; the voice was distorted by electronics and static.

In the dim gloom, Sahid's voice floated up from the floor like mist. "Richards, how did you injure your finger?"

She wasn't sure at first if she wanted to tell him what had happened. He might think she was crazy—a hysterical female who had finally let the job get the better of her. It was bad enough she had asked him to sleep in here with her, as if she was a child afraid of the dark. "Something bit me."

It was quiet. Then Sahid spoke again. "What is your first name?"

That wasn't what she was expecting. "Anna."

"And my name is Michael. We only have one more night on board this ship, Anna, then we can go home."

Anna closed her eyes. Home. And she dreamt that she went back to her little apartment and there was nothing there, that everything had been salvaged, taken away. She could even see the little dents in the rug where the furniture had once stood.

There was a message in red ink on the wall of her bedroom, the room that stilled smelled of her scent; it said: *Anna, we are waiting.*

She began to cry.

Anna woke with a start; someone was in the cabin with them. Michael was awake as well, pressed up against the bunk where Anna slept. The intruder stood in the doorway, not saying anything. Anna could see he was a man from his height and strong shoulders; he was in the uniform of the company.

Anna heard a clicking sound and saw that at the man's heels a little red dog gambolled, jumping up in the air and making snapping noises with its jaws, as if it were trying to get his attention. Anna switched on the nightlight above the bed and the man vanished. There was no dog either, but for just a moment Anna heard the dog's jaws snapping, as if he were next to her ear. Voices were coming out of the headset.

"Richards, get down to the main lounge, there's an emergency." The voice sounded frantic and garbled; there was yelling in the background.

Anna and Michael both stood up and moved to the door, Michael pausing only long enough to grab his medic kit. They ran through the empty corridors of the ship. Anna felt the cold of the metal beneath the carpet that lined the halls on her feet and wished she had put some shoes on. The idea of an emergency was unreal. It was too solid a word to fit with the things she had experienced since coming on the ship. It would be nothing, Thompson wanting the crew to see her in her pyjamas, a way to catch Michael in her room, ordinary.

In the main lounge, the rest of the crew was gathered. No one made a comment about Richards and Sahid coming in together; they were all huddled around a chair. Thompson was sitting in it, a blanket wrapped around his shoulders, his face pale, lips faintly blue. There was blood splatter across his pants.

"What happened?" Richards asked the crewmember closest to her, but he just shook his head. She stepped in closer.

Thompson saw her and began to babble, "It was a dog, a little dog."

One of the other members of the crew, whose name she vaguely remembered as Davies said, "We were packing up the last crates on the flight deck when this little . . ." Here he paused as if not sure what word to use, ". . . dog, I guess, ran in. It ran up to Thompson and started sniffing at his pant legs. Thompson started chasing it and we followed, running down the hall toward the crew cabins. I saw Thompson reach out to grab it, and it looked as if the dog thing turned around and snapped at him and Thompson began to scream and fell on the floor. We had a helluva time getting him in here."

Thompson was eyeing Richards still. "It burned me, it burned me." He held up his hands so that she could see. Their centres were raw and bloody with blackened edges.

Sahid stepped up and took one of them. Thompson let him, his hand lying in Sahid's like fat cut from a piece of pork. In the singed areas of the wound there were coarse black hairs. Thompson began to keen, swaying back and forth in his chair.

Sahid took a syringe and a bottle from his kit. He filled the needle and asked Anna to hold Thompson's arm.

Thompson turned to Anna as the liquid entered his veins and said, "It talked to me, it talked to me." When Sahid removed the needle, Thompson turned to him and said, "It told me I was going to die, it said I was going to die."

Sahid put the used needle and bottle in a plastic

bag. "We're all going to die, Thompson. It wasn't telling you anything you didn't all ready know."

Thompson looked at Sahid for moment as if pleading with him. "Are we? But I don't want to." And his handsome empty head slumped forward onto his chest.

Sahid disinfected and bandaged the wounds on Thompson's hands quickly. Then three of the other crewmembers half carried, half dragged him over to the lounge sofa and laid him on it.

"He'll sleep through the night," Sahid said as he and Richards stood looking down at Thompson, reduced to a childlike harmless status with his bandaged hands like the white paws of a puppy and his golden lashes. "Shall we stay here tonight with the rest of the crew, Anna?"

Anna looked around the room. Some of the crew were asleep in chairs or on the floor; the rest talked quietly, heads bent together as if imparting deep secrets to one another.

"Yes, I think so," she said. "But sit close to me."

The next morning, Thompson awoke roaring with pain and fear. Sahid gave him another shot and he drifted off again. The company shuttle arrived and the crew worked quickly, loading it with crates and equipment, everyone trying not to look in the dark empty corners of the ship where those things had once stood. Michael and Anna went back to the cabin they had spent part of the night in before. They rolled up their sleeping bags, dressed and gathered their packs together. Neither of them spoke of the man and dog in the doorway, or the cabin next door. When Anna passed it on her way down the corridor, she remembered her dream and a deep sorrow swept over her. Then, for just a minute, she thought she heard a scratching at the cabin's shut door, as if an animal trapped inside was trying to get out. She started running to catch up with Michael and didn't look back.

Thompson was put on a stretcher and loaded onto the shuttle just like the rest of the salvage.

Anna and Michael sat in seats across from each other. They didn't talk and Anna stared out the window at the ship rapidly getting smaller, as if it were pulling away from them to disappear into the endless black, not the other way around. She could see nothing above her, nothing below her but deep ebony and understood that she was floating here in this shuttle, at this time, on faith in the manipulations of humans.

"We are going to die, aren't we, Michael?" She didn't turn to him, didn't turn from the window. He reached over and gently closed the shade.

Acknowledgements

Thank you to Sandra Kasturi who is a great editor, writer and friend and encouraged me from the beginning in my dream to write ghost stories. Thanks to Brett Savory who rocks in all ways. Love to my family on Lincoln Road for the ghost stories around the dining room table, and to the men of GLPARS for taking me on a ghost hunt. Couldn't have finished this book without the support of my partner in crime at Tightrope, Shirarose, who lets me buy a little time to write, or the support of my friends, you know who you are, if not, call me and we'll talk.

Thank you to the OAC for supporting an early draft of this book through the Writer's Works in Progress grant, and to the OAC and TAC for grants to allow me to focus on writing.

Finally, all love and thanks to Misha and David, my two polestars who spur me on in so many ways and mean the world to me.

About the Author

Halli Villegas is the author of three collections of poetry, *Red Promises*, *In the Silence Absence Makes* and *The Human Cannonball*, and several anthology pieces. She has published online erotica under a pen name. Her poetry and prose have appeared in places such as the *LRC*, *Exile*, *Kiss Machine*, *Pagitica* and, most recently, *Variety Crossings* and *The Windsor Review*. Halli has received funding for her writing from the OAC Works in Progress in 2006, the TAC mid-level writers in 2007 and 2009, and the OAC Works in Progress in 2009.

She is also the publisher of Tightrope Books and the administrative director of the Rowers Pub Reading Series.

Copyrights